Acclaim for JEANETTE WINTERSON'S

Written on the Body

"Arresting . . . a lush story of passion . . . an affirmation of the freedom to cast off all prescriptions: social, moral, existential, sexual—and in the writing—aesthetic and literary. We are cut off from our assumptions and groomed to enter Winterson's unsettling polymorphous world."
—Richard Eder, *Los Angeles Times Book Review*

"Winterson's skill with fable and fantasy is not just brilliant plumage in this book. . . . [Her] representations of desire go far beyond male/female; she moves past all dichotomies into a register of sexual imagery where the body is weapon, flora, fauna, weather, animal, geography, prison, food, light, nest, jagged edge: it is the body as whole world. In this novel she found the spot where the Great Chain of Being breaks and none of us know what will become of us, or where we fit."
—*Village Voice*

"Brilliant . . . Stunning passages of romantic rapture [and] anguished tenderness. *Written on the Body* takes on a certain cinematic splendor."
—*Boston Globe*

"A bold, controversial new novel . . . the story of a white hot passion. [Winterson] is regularly singled out as the most talented writer of her generation."
—*Mirabella*

"This is a story of the heart, a foray into the emotional imagination. The language [is] elegiac, passionate, reverential, with echoes of the Song of Solomon. Moving and compassionate, a love letter as much as a love story."
—*Harper's Bazaar*

"A knockout . . . sexual ecstasy is described with surreal sensuality. Fascinating [and] unforgettable. Winterson writes about the state of passion, casting an obsessed eye on the body, mapping its every detail and secret place. Winterson is an exciting writer. She has literary talent of a high order."
—*Vogue*

"A serious display of literary talent. Winterson broods entertainingly about passion, loyalty, beauty, disease, and decay in a language that draws on Donne, Shakespeare, snippets from anatomy texts, and her own unabashed sexiness. A tour de force, with bravado and heart."
—*Entertainment Weekly*

"Intense . . . an anatomy of sexual love: Winterson takes an interest in the physiology of love, in the ways it makes the body feel and change, in the body's centrality to love. She is a scintillating writer, witty, inventive with language."
—*USA Today*

JEANETTE WINTERSON

Written on the Body

Jeanette Winterson was born in Lancashire in 1959, grew up in Lancashire, and now lives in London. *Oranges Are Not the Only Fruit* won the Whitbread Award for best first novel; her adaptation of *Oranges* for BBC television has won her prizes around the world, including a British Academy of Film and Television Arts award for best drama. Her novel *The Passion* won the John Llewellyn Rhys Memorial Prize. When *Sexing the Cherry* was published in 1989, Jeanette Winterson received the E. M. Forster Award from the American Academy and Institute of Arts and Letters. Her most recent work is *The World and Other Places,* a collection of short stories.

INTERNATIONAL

ALSO BY JEANETTE WINTERSON

WRITTEN ON THE BODY

Jeanette Winterson

VINTAGE INTERNATIONAL
Vintage Books
A Division of Random House, Inc.
New York

FIRST VINTAGE INTERNATIONAL EDITION, FEBRUARY 1994

Library of Congress Cataloging-in-Publication Data
Winterson, Jeanette, 1959–
Written on the body/Jeanette Winterson —1st Vintage international ed
p cm
ISBN 0-679-74447-9
1 Married women—England—Fiction I Title
[PR6073 I558W56 1994]
823´ 914—dc20   93-23335
CIP

Author photograph © Jillian Edelstein

Manufactured in the United States of America
3579C864

for Peggy Reynolds with love

My thanks are due to Don and Ruth Rendell whose hospitality gave me the space to work. To Philippa Brewster for her editorial inspiration. To all those at Jonathan Cape who have worked so hard to produce this book.

Why is the measure of love loss?

It hasn't rained for three months. The trees are pros-pecting underground, sending reserves of roots into the dry ground, roots like razors to open any artery water-fat. The grapes have withered on the vine. What should be plump and firm, resisting the touch to give itself in the mouth, is spongy and blistered. Not this year the pleasure of rolling blue grapes between finger and thumb juicing my palm with musk. Even the wasps avoid the thin brown dribble. Even the wasps this year. It was not always so.

I am thinking of a certain September: Wood pigeon Red Admiral Yellow Harvest Orange Night. You said, 'I love you.' Why is it that the most unoriginal thing we can say to one another is still the thing we long to hear? 'I love you' is always a quotation. You did not say it first and neither did I, yet when you say it and when I say it we speak like savages who have found three words and worship them. I did worship them but now I am alone on a rock hewn out of my own body.

CALIBAN   You taught me language and my profit on't is
           I know how to curse. The red plague rid you
           For learning me your language.

Love demands expression. It will not stay still, stay silent, be good, be modest, be seen and not heard, no. It will break out in tongues of praise, the high note that smashes the glass and spills the liquid. It is no

≈ 9 ≈

conservationist love. It is a big game hunter and you are the game. A curse on this game. How can you stick at a game when the rules keep changing? I shall call myself Alice and play croquet with the flamingoes. In Wonderland everyone cheats and love is Wonderland isn't it? Love makes the world go round. Love is blind. All you need is love. Nobody ever died of a broken heart. You'll get over it. It'll be different when we're married. Think of the children. Time's a great healer. Still waiting for Mr Right? Miss Right? and maybe all the little Rights?

It's the clichés that cause the trouble. A precise emotion seeks a precise expression. If what I feel is not precise then should I call it love? It is so terrifying, love, that all I can do is shove it under a dump bin of pink cuddly toys and send myself a greetings card saying 'Congratulations on your Engagement'. But I am not engaged I am deeply distracted. I am desperately looking the other way so that love won't see me. I want the diluted version, the sloppy language, the insignificant gestures. The saggy armchair of clichés. It's all right, millions of bottoms have sat here before me. The springs are well worn, the fabric smelly and familiar. I don't have to be frightened, look, my grandma and grandad did it, he in a stiff collar and club tie, she in white muslin straining a little at the life beneath. They did it, my parents did it, now I will do it won't I, arms outstretched, not to hold you, just to keep my balance, sleepwalking to that armchair. How happy we will be. How happy everyone will be. And they all lived happily ever after.

It was a hot August Sunday. I paddled through the shallows of the river where the little fishes dare their belly at the sun. On either side of the river the proper green of the grass had given way to a psychedelic splash-painting of virulent Lycra cycling shorts and Hawaiian shirts made in Taiwan. They were grouped the way families like to group; dad with the paper propped on his overhang, mum sagging over the thermos. Kids thin as seaside rock sticks and seaside rock pink. Mum saw you go in and heaved herself off the stripey fold-out camping stool. 'You should be ashamed of yourself. There's families out here.'

You laughed and waved, your body bright beneath the clear green water, its shape fitting your shape, holding you, faithful to you. You turned on your back and your nipples grazed the surface of the river and the river decorated your hair with beads. You are creamy but for your hair your red hair that flanks you on either side.

'I'll get my husband to see to you. George come here. George come here.'

'Can't you see I'm watching television?' said George without turning round.

You stood up and the water fell from you in silver streams. I didn't think, I waded in and kissed you. You put your arms around my burning back. You said, 'There's nobody here but us.'

I looked up and the banks were empty.

You were careful not to say those words that soon became our private altar. I had said them many times before, dropping them like coins into a wishing well, hoping they would make me come true. I had said them many times before but not to you. I had given them as forget-me-nots to girls who should have known better. I had used them as bullets and barter. I don't like to think of myself as an insincere person but if I say I love you and I don't mean it then what else am I? Will I cherish

≈ 11 ≈

you, adore you, make way for you, make myself better
for you, look at you and always see you, tell you the
truth? And if love is not those things then what things?

August. We were arguing. You want love to be like
this every day don't you? 92 degrees even in the shade.
This intensity, this heat, sun like a disc-saw through your
body. Is it because you come from Australia?

You didn't answer, just held my hot hand in your
cool fingers and strode on easy in linen and silk. I felt
ridiculous. I was wearing a pair of shorts with RECYCLE
tattooed across one leg. I remembered vaguely that I had
once had a girlfriend who thought it rude to wear shorts
in front of public monuments. When we met I tethered
my bike at Charing Cross and changed in the toilets before
meeting her by Nelson's Column.

'Why bother?' I said. 'He only had one eye.'

'I've got two,' she said and kissed me. Wrong to
seal illogic with a kiss but I do it myself all the time.

You didn't answer. Why do human beings need
answers? Partly I suppose because without one, almost
any one, the question itself soon sounds silly. Try standing in front of a class and asking what is the capital of
Canada. The eyes stare back at you, indifferent, hostile,
some of them look the other way. You say it again.
'What is the capital of Canada?' While you wait in the
silence, absolutely the victim, your own mind doubts
itself. What *is* the capital of Canada? Why Ottawa and
not Montreal? Montreal is much nicer, they do a better
espresso, you have a friend who lives there. Anyway,
who cares what the capital is, they'll probably change it
next year. Perhaps Gloria will be at the swimming pool
tonight. And so on.

Bigger questions, questions with more than one answer, questions without an answer are harder to cope with in silence. Once asked they do not evaporate and leave the mind to its serener musings. Once asked they gain dimension and texture, trip you on the stairs, wake you at night-time. A black hole sucks up its surroundings and even light never escapes. Better then to ask no questions? Better then to be a contented pig than an unhappy Socrates? Since factory farming is tougher on pigs than it is on philosophers I'll take a chance.

We walked back to our rented room and lay on one of the single beds. In rented rooms from Brighton to Bangkok, the bedspread never matches the carpet and the towels are too thin. I put one underneath you to save the sheet. You were bleeding.

We had rented this room, your idea, to try to be together for more than dinner or a night or a cup of tea behind the library. You were still married and although I don't have many scruples I've learned to have some about that blessed state. I used to think of marriage as a plate-glass window just begging for a brick. The self-exhibition, the self-satisfaction, smarminess, tightness, tight-arsedness. The way married couples go out in fours like a pantomime horse, the men walking together at the front, the women trailing a little way behind. The men fetching the gin and tonics from the bar while the women take their handbags to the toilet. It doesn't have to be like that but mostly it is. I've been through a lot of marriages. Not down the aisle but always up the stairs. I began to realise I was hearing the same story every time. It went like this.

Interior. Afternoon.
A bedroom. Curtains half drawn. Bedclothes thrown back.
A naked woman of a certain age lies on the bed looking at the
ceiling. She wants to say something. She's finding it difficult.
A cassette recorder is playing Ella Fitzgerald, 'Lady Sings the
Blues'.

NAKED WOMAN   I wanted to tell you that I don't usually
do this. I suppose it's called committing
adultery. (*She laughs.*) I've never done it
before. I don't think I could do it again.
With someone else that is. Oh I want to
do it again with you. Over and over
again. (*She rolls on to her stomach.*) I
love my husband you know. I do love
him. He's not like other men. I couldn't
have married him if he was. He's different, we've got a lot in common. We
talk.

Her lover runs a finger over the bare lips of the naked
woman. Lies over her, looks at her. The lover says nothing.

NAKED WOMAN   If I hadn't met you I suppose I *would*
be looking for something. I might have
done a degree at the Open University. I
wasn't thinking of this. I never wanted
to give him a moment's worry. That's
why I can't tell him. Why we must be
careful. I don't want to be cruel and
selfish. You do see that don't you?

Her lover gets up and goes to the toilet. The naked woman
raises herself on her elbow and continues her monologue in the
direction of the en suite bathroom.

NAKED WOMAN   Don't be long darling. (*She pauses.*) I've
tried to get you out of my head but I
can't seem to get you out of my flesh.
I think about your body day and night.
When I try to read it's you I'm reading.
When I sit down to eat it's you I'm eating. When he touches me I think about
you. I'm a middle-aged happily married
woman and all I can see is your face.
What have you done to me?

Cut to en suite bathroom. The lover is crying. End scene.

It's flattering to believe that you and only you, the
great lover, could have done this. That without you, the
marriage, incomplete though it is, pathetic in many ways,
would have thrived on its meagre diet and if not thrived at
least not shrivelled. It has shrivelled, lies limp and unused,
the shell of a marriage, its inhabitants both fled. People
collect shells though don't they? They spend money on
them and display them on their window ledges. Other
people admire them. I've seen some very famous shells
and blown into the hollows of many more. Where I've
left cracking too severe to mend the owners have simply
turned the bad part to the shade.

See? Even here in this private place my syntax has
fallen prey to the deceit. It was not I who did those
things; cut the knot, jemmied the lock, made off with
goods not mine to take. The door was open. True, she
didn't exactly open it herself. Her butler opened it for her.
His name was Boredom. She said, 'Boredom, fetch me a
plaything.' He said, 'Very good ma'am,' and putting on
his white gloves so that the fingerprints would not show

he tapped at my heart and I thought he said his name was Love.

You think I'm trying to wriggle out of my responsibilities? No, I know what I did and what I was doing at the time. But I didn't walk down the aisle, queue up at the Registry Office and swear to be faithful unto death. I wouldn't dare. I didn't say, 'With this ring I thee wed.' I didn't say, 'With my body I thee worship.' How can you say that to one person and gladly fuck another? Shouldn't you take that vow and break it the way you made it, in the open air?

Odd that marriage, a public display and free to all, gives way to that most secret of liaisons, an adulterous affair.

I had a lover once, her name was Bathsheba. She was a happily married woman. I began to feel as though we were crewing a submarine. We couldn't tell our friends, at least she couldn't tell hers because they were his too. I couldn't tell mine because she asked me not to do so. We sank lower and lower in our love-lined lead-lined coffin. Telling the truth, she said, was a luxury we could not afford and so lying became a virtue, an economy we had to practise. Telling the truth was hurtful and so lying became a good deed. One day I said, 'I'm going to tell him myself.' This was after two years, two years where I thought that she must leave eventually eventually, eventually. The word she used was 'monstrous'. Monstrous to tell him. Monstrous. I thought of Caliban chained to his pitted rock. 'The red plague rid you for learning me your language.'

Later, when I was freed from her world of double meanings and masonic signs I did turn thief. I had never stolen from her, she had spread her wares on a blanket and asked me to choose. (There was a price but in brackets.) When we were over, I wanted my letters back. My copyright she said but her property. She had said the same about my body. Perhaps it was wrong to climb into her lumber-room and take back the last of myself. They were easy to find, stuffed into a large padded bag, bearing the message on an Oxfam label that they were to be returned to me in the event of her death. A nice touch; he would no doubt have read them but then she would not have been there to take the consequences. And would I have read them? Probably. A nice touch.

I took them into the garden and burned them one by one and I thought how easy it is to destroy the past and how difficult to forget it.

Did I say this has happened to me again and again? You will think I have been constantly in and out of married women's lumber-rooms. I have a head for heights it's true, but no stomach for the depths. Strange then to have plumbed so many.

We lay on our bed in the rented room and I fed you plums the colour of bruises. Nature is fecund but fickle. One year she leaves you to starve, the next year she kills you with love. That year the branches were torn beneath the weight, this year they sing in the wind. There are no ripe plums in August. Have I got it wrong, this hesitant chronology? Perhaps I should call it Emma Bovary's eyes or Jane Eyre's dress. I don't know. I'm in another rented room now trying to find the place to go back to where things went wrong. Where I went wrong. You were driving but I was lost in my own navigation.

Nevertheless I will push on. There were plums and I broke them over you.

You said, 'Why do I frighten you?'

Frighten me? Yes you do frighten me. You act as though we will be together for ever. You act as though there is infinite pleasure and time without end. How can I know that? My experience has been that time always ends. In theory you are right, the quantum physicists are right, the romantics and the religious are right. Time without end. In practice we both wear a watch. If I rush at this relationship it's because I fear for it. I fear you have a door I cannot see and that any minute now the door will open and you'll be gone. Then what? Then what as I bang the walls like the Inquisition searching for a saint? Where will I find the secret passage? For me it'll just be the same four walls.

You said, 'I'm going to leave.'

I thought, Yes, of course you are, you're going back to the shell. I'm an idiot. I've done it again and I said I'd never do it again.

You said, 'I told him before we came away. I've told him I won't change my mind even if you change yours.'

This is the wrong script. This is the moment where I'm supposed to be self-righteous and angry. This is the moment where you're supposed to flood with tears and tell me how hard it is to say these things and what can you do and what can you do and will I hate you and yes you know I'll hate you and there are no question marks in this speech because it's a fait accompli.

But you are gazing at me the way God gazed at Adam and I am embarrassed by your look of love and possession and pride. I want to go now and cover myself with fig leaves. It's a sin this not being ready, this not being up to it.

You said, 'I love you and my love for you makes any other life a lie.'

Can this be true, this simple obvious message, or am I like those shipwrecked mariners who seize an empty bottle and eagerly read out what isn't there? And yet you are there, here, sprung like a genie to ten times your natural size, towering over me, holding me in your arms like mountain sides. Your red hair is blazing and you are saying, 'Make three wishes and they shall all come true. Make three hundred and I will honour every one.'

What did we do that night? We must have walked wrapped around each other to a café that was a church and eaten a Greek salad that tasted like a wedding feast. We met a cat who agreed to be best man and our bouquets were Ragged Robin from the side of the canal. We had about two thousand guests, mostly midges and we felt we were old enough to give ourselves away. It would have been good to have lain down there and made love under the moon but the truth is that, outside of the movies and Country and Western songs, the outdoors is an itchy business.

I had a girlfriend once who was addicted to starlit nights. She thought beds belonged in hospitals. Anywhere she could do it that wasn't pre-sprung was sexy. Show her a duvet and she switched on the television. I coped with this on campsites and in canoes, British Rail and Aeroflot. I bought a futon, eventually a gym mat. I had to lay extra-thick carpet on the floor. I took to carrying a tartan rug wherever I went, like a far-out member of the Scottish Nationalist Party. Eventually, back at the doctor's for the fifth time having a thistle removed, he said to me, 'You know, love is a very beautiful thing but there are clinics for people like you.' Now, it's a serious matter to have 'PERVERT' written on your NHS file and some indignities are just a romance too far. We had to say goodbye and although there were some things about her that I missed it was pleasant to walk in the country again without seeing every bush and shrub as a potential assailant.

Louise, in this single bed, between these garish sheets, I will find a map as likely as any treasure hunt. I will explore you and mine you and you will redraw me according to your will. We shall cross one another's boundaries and make ourselves one nation. Scoop me in your hands for I am good soil. Eat of me and let me be sweet.

June. The wettest June on record. We made love every day. We were happy like colts, flagrant like rabbits, dove-innocent in our pursuit of pleasure. Neither of us thought about it and we had no time to discuss it. The time we had we used. Those brief days and briefer hours were small offerings to a god who would not be appeased by burning flesh. We consumed each other and went hungry again. There were patches of relief, moments of tranquillity as still as an artificial lake, but always behind us the roaring tide.

There are people who say that sex isn't important in a relationship. That friendship and getting along are what coast you through the years. No doubt this is a faithful testimony but is it a true one? I had come to this feeling myself. One does after years of playing the Lothario and seeing nothing but an empty bank account and a pile of yellowing love-notes like IOUs. I had done to death the candles and champagne, the roses, the dawn breakfasts, the transatlantic telephone calls and the impulsive plane rides. I had done all of that to escape the cocoa and hot water bottles. And I had done all of that because I thought the fiery furnace must be better than central heating. I suppose I couldn't admit that I was trapped in a cliché every bit as redundant as my parents' roses round the door. I was looking for the perfect coupling; the never-sleep non-stop mighty orgasm. Ecstasy without end. I was deep in the slop-bucket of romance. Sure my bucket was a bit racier than most, I've always had a sports car, but you can't rev your way out of real life. That home girl gonna get you in the end. This is how it happened.

I was in the last spasms of an affair with a Dutch girl called Inge. She was a committed romantic and an anarcha-feminist. This was hard for her because it meant she couldn't blow up beautiful buildings. She knew the Eiffel Tower was a hideous symbol of phallic oppression but when ordered by her commander to detonate the lift so that no-one should unthinkingly scale an erection, her mind filled with young romantics gazing over Paris and opening aerograms that said Je t'aime.

We went to the Louvre to see a Renoir exhibition. Inge wore her guerilla cap and boots in case she should be mistaken for a tourist. She justified her ticket price as 'political research'. 'Look at those nudes,' she said, although I needed no urging. 'Bodies everywhere, naked, abused, exposed. Do you know how much those models were paid? Hardly the price of a baguette. I should rip the canvases from their frames and go to prison crying "Vive la resistance".'

Renoir's nudes are not at all the world's finest nudes, but

even so, when we came to his painting of La Boulangère, Inge wept. She said, 'I hate it because it moves me.' I didn't say that thus are tyrants made, I said, 'It's not the painter, it's the paint. Forget Renoir, hold on to the picture.'

She said, 'Don't you know that Renoir claimed he painted with his penis?'

'Don't worry,' I said. 'He did. When he died they found nothing between his balls but an old brush.'

'You're making it up.'

Am I?

Eventually we resolved Inge's aesthetic crisis by taking her Semtex to a number of carefully chosen urinals. They were all concrete Nissan huts, absolutely ugly and clearly functionaries of the penis. She said I wasn't fit to be an assistant in the fight towards a new matriarchy because I had QUALMS. This was a capital offence. Nevertheless, it wasn't the terrorism that flung us apart, it was the pigeons . . .

My job was to go into the urinals wearing one of Inge's stockings over my head. That in itself might not have attracted much attention, men's toilets are fairly liberal places, but then I had to warn the row of guys that they were in danger of having their balls blown off unless they left at once. A typical occasion would be to find five of them, cocks in hand, staring at the brown-streaked porcelain as though it were the Holy Grail. Why *do* men like doing everything together? I said (quoting Inge), 'This urinal is a symbol of patriarchy and must be destroyed.' Then (in my own voice), 'My girlfriend has just wired up the Semtex, would you mind finishing off?'

What would you do under the circumstances? Wouldn't impending castration followed by certain death be enough to cause a normal man to wipe his dick and run for it? They didn't. Over and over again they didn't, just flicked the drops contemptuously and swapped tips about the racing. I'm a mild-mannered sort but I don't like rudeness. On the job I found it helped to carry a gun.

I pulled it out of the waistband of my RECYCLE shorts (yes I've had them a long time) and pointed the barrel at the nearest dangle. This caused a bit of a stir and one said, 'You a loony or something?' He said that but he zipped his flies and buzzed off. 'Hands up *boys*,' I said. 'No, don't touch it, it'll have to dry in the wind.'

At that moment I heard the opening bars of 'Strangers in the Night'. It was Inge's signal to say we had five minutes ready or not. I motioned my doubting John Thomases through the door and broke into a run. I had to get into the mobile burger-bar Inge used as a hide-out. I threw myself in beside her and looked back from between the bread rolls. It was a beautiful explosion. A splendid explosion, much too good for a load of demi-johns. We were alone on the edge of the world, terrorists fighting the good fight for a fairer society. I thought I loved her and then came the pigeons.

She forbade me to telephone her. She said that telephones were for Receptionists, that is, women without status. I said, fine, I'll write. Wrong, she said. The Postal Service was run by despots who exploited non-union labour. What were we to do? I didn't want to live in Holland. She didn't want to live in London. How could we communicate?

Pigeons, she said.

That is how I came to rent the attic floor of the Pimlico Women's Institute. I don't feel a great deal about the Women's Institute either way, they were the first to campaign against aerosols that contain CFCs and they make a mean Victoria sponge but I don't really care. The point was that their attic faced roughly in the direction of Amsterdam.

I can tell by now that you are wondering whether I can be trusted as a narrator. Why didn't I dump Inge and head for a Singles Bar? The answer is her breasts.

They were not marvellously upright, the kind women wear as epaulettes, as a mark of rank. Neither were they pubescent playboy fantasies. They had done their share of time and begun to submit to gravity's insistence. The flesh was brown, the aureoles browner still, nipples bead black. My gypsy sisters I called them, though not to her. I had idolised them simply and unequivocally, not as a mother substitute nor a womb trauma, but for themselves. Freud didn't always get it right. Sometimes a breast is a breast is a breast.

Half a dozen times I picked up the phone. Six times I put it down again. Probably she wouldn't have answered. She would have had it disconnected but for her mother in Rotterdam. She never did explain how she would know it was her mother and not a Receptionist. How she would know it was a Receptionist and not me. I wanted to talk to her.

The pigeons, Adam, Eve and Kissmequick, couldn't manage Holland. Eve got as far as Folkestone. Adam dropped out and went to live in Trafalgar Square, another victory to Nelson. Kissmequick was scared of heights, a drawback for a bird, but the WI took him in as their mascot and rechristened him Boadicea. If he has not died yet he is still living. I don't know what happened to Inge's birds. They never came to me.

Then I met Jacqueline.

I had to lay a carpet in my new flat so a couple of friends came over to help. They brought Jacqueline. She was the mistress of one of them confidante of both. A sort of household pet. She traded sex and sympathy for £50 to tide her over the weekend and a square meal on Sunday. It was a civilised if brutal arrangement.

I had bought a new flat to start again from a nasty love affair that had given me the clap. Nothing wrong with my organs, this was emotional clap. I had to keep my heart to myself in case I infected somebody. The flat was large and derelict. I hoped I might rebuild it and myself at the same time. The clap-giver was still with her husband in their tasteful house but she'd slipped me £10,000 to help finance my purchase. Give/Lend was how she put it. Blood money was how I put it. She was buying off what conscience she had. I intended never to see her again. Unfortunately she was my dentist.

Jacqueline worked at the Zoo. She worked with small furry things that wouldn't be nice to visitors. Visitors who have paid £5 don't have a lot of patience for small furry things who are frightened and want to hide. It was Jacqueline's job to make everything bright and shiny again. She was good with parents, good with children, good with animals, good with disturbed things of every kind. She was good with me.

When she arrived, smart but not trendy, made-up but not conspicuously, her voice flat, her spectacles clownish, I thought, I have nothing to say to this woman. After Inge, and my brief addictive return to Bathsheba the dentist, I could not foresee pleasure in any woman, especially not one who had been victimised by her hairdresser. I thought, You can make the tea and I'll joke with my old friends about the perils of a broken heart and then you shall all three go home together happy in your good deed while I open a can of lentils and listen to 'Science Now' on the wireless.

Poor me. There's nothing so sweet as wallowing in it is there? Wallowing is sex for depressives. I should remember my grandmother's motto offered to the suffering as pastoral care. Not for her the painful dilemma, the agonised choice, 'Either shit or get off the pot.' That's right. At least I was between turds.

Jacqueline made me a sandwich and asked if I had any washing-up I'd like done. She came the next day and the day after that. She told me all about the problems facing lemurs in the Zoo. She brought her own mop. She worked nine to five Monday to Friday, drove a Mini and got her reading from book clubs. She exhibited no fetishes, foibles, freak-outs or fuck-ups. Above all she was single and she had always been single. No children and no husband.

I considered her. I didn't love her and I didn't want to love her. I didn't desire her and I could not imagine desiring her. These were all points in her favour. I had lately learned that another way of writing FALL IN LOVE is WALK THE PLANK. I was tired of balancing blindfold on a slender beam, one slip and into the unplumbed sea. I wanted the clichés, the armchair. I wanted the broad road and twenty-twenty vision. What's wrong with that? It's called growing up. Maybe most people gloss their comforts with a patina of romance but it soon wears off. They're in it for the long haul; the expanding waistline and the little semi in the suburbs. What's wrong with that? Late-night TV and snoring side by side into the millennium. Till death us do part. Anniversary darling? What's wrong with that?

I considered her. She had no expensive tastes, knew

nothing about wine, never wanted to be taken to the opera and had fallen in love with me. I had no money and no morale. It was a marriage made in heaven.

We agreed that we were good for each other whilst sitting in her Mini eating a Chinese take-away. It was a cloudy night so we couldn't look at the stars and besides, she had to be up for work at half past seven. I don't think we even slept together that night. It was the next night, freezing cold in November and I'd lit the fire. I'd arranged a few flowers because I like to do that anyway but when it came to getting out the tablecloth and finding the good glasses I couldn't be bothered. 'We're not like that,' I told myself. 'What we have is simple and ordinary. That's why I like it. It's worth lies in its neatness. No more sprawling life for me. This is container gardening.'

Over the months that followed my mind healed and I no longer moped and groaned over lost love and impossible choices. I had survived shipwreck and I liked my new island with hot and cold running water and regular visits from the milkman. I became an apostle of ordinariness. I lectured my friends on the virtues of the humdrum, praised the gentle bands of my existence and felt that for the first time I had come to know what everyone told me I would know; that passion is for holidays, not homecoming.

My friends were more circumspect than me. They regarded Jacqueline with a wary approval, regarding me as one might a mental patient who has been behaving for a few months. A few months? More like a year. I was rigorous, hard working and . . . and . . . what was that word beginning with B?

'You're bored,' my friend said.

I protested with all the fervour of a teetotaller caught glancing at the bottle. I was content. I had settled down.

'Still having sex?'

'Not much. It doesn't matter you know. We do now and then. When we both feel like it. We work hard. We don't have a lot of time.'

'Do you look at her and want her? Do you look at her and notice her?'

I lost my temper. Why was my happily settled, happily happy Heidi house coming under fire from a friend who had put up with all my broken hearts without a word of reproach? I struggled in my mind with all kinds of defences. Should I be hurt? Surprised? Should I laugh it off? I wanted to say something cruel to expiate my anger and to justify myself. But it's difficult with old friends; difficult because it's so easy. You know one another as well as lovers do and you have had less to pretend about. I poured myself a drink and shrugged.

'Nothing's perfect.'

The worm in the bud. So what? Most buds do have worms. You spray, you fuss, you hope the hole won't be too big and you pray for sunshine. Just let the flower bloom and no-one will notice the ragged edges. I thought that about me and Jacqueline. I was desperate to tend us. I wanted the relationship to work for not very noble reasons; after all it was my last ditch. No more racing for me. She loved me too, yes she did, in her uncomplicated undemanding way. She never bothered me when I said, 'Don't bother me,' and she didn't cry when I shouted at her. In fact she shouted back. She treated me like a big cat in the Zoo. She was very proud of me.

My friend said, 'Pick on someone your own size.'

And then I met Louise.

If I were painting Louise I'd paint her hair as a swarm

of butterflies. A million Red Admirals in a halo of movement and light. There are plenty of legends about women turning into trees but are there any about trees turning into women? Is it odd to say that your lover reminds you of a tree? Well she does, it's the way her hair fills with wind and sweeps out around her head. Very often I expect her to rustle. She doesn't rustle but her flesh has the moonlit shade of a silver birch. Would I had a hedge of such saplings naked and unadorned.

At first it didn't matter. We got on well as a threesome. Louise was kind to Jacqueline and never tried to come between us even as a friend. In any case, why should she? She was happily married and had been so for ten years. I had met her husband, a doctor with just the right bedside manner, he was unremarkable but that is not a vice.

'She's very beautiful isn't she?' said Jacqueline.

'Who?'

'Louise.'

'Yes, yes, I suppose she is if you like that sort of thing.'

'Do you like that sort of thing?'

'I like Louise yes. You know I do. So do you.'

'Yes.'

She went back to her *World Wildlife* magazine and I went for a walk.

I was only going for a walk, any old walk, nowhere special walk, but I found myself outside Louise's front door. Dear me. What am I doing here? I was going the other way.

I rang the bell. Louise answered. Her husband Elgin was in his study playing a computer game called HOSPITAL. You get to operate on a patient who shouts at you if you do it wrong.

'Hello Louise. I was passing so I thought I might pop in.'

Pop in. What a ridiculous phrase. What am I, a cuckoo clock?

We went down the hall together. Elgin shot his head out of the study door. 'Hello there. Hello, hello, very nice. Be with you, little problem with the liver, can't seem to find it.'

In the kitchen Louise gave me a drink and a chaste kiss on the cheek. It would have been chaste if she'd taken her lips away at once, but instead she offered the obligatory peck and moved her lips imperceptibly over the spot. It took about twice as long as it should have done, which was still no time at all. Unless it's your cheek. Unless you're already thinking that way and wondering if someone else is thinking that way too. She gave no sign. I gave no sign. We sat and talked and listened to music and I didn't notice the dark or the lateness of the hour or the bottle now empty or my stomach now empty. The phone rang, obscenely loud, we both jumped. Louise answered it in her careful way, listened a moment then passed it over to me. It was Jacqueline. She said, very sad, not reproachful, but sad, 'I wondered where you were. It's nearly midnight. I wondered where you were.'

'I'm sorry. I'll get a cab now. I'll be with you soon.'

I stood up and smiled. 'Can you get me a cab?'

'I'll drive you,' she said. 'It would be nice to see Jacqueline.'

We didn't talk on the way back. The streets were quiet, there was nothing on the road. We pulled up outside my flat and I said thank you and we made an arrangement to meet for tea the following week and then she said, 'I've got tickets for the opera tomorrow night. Elgin can't come. Will you come?'

'We're supposed to be having a night in tomorrow.'
She nodded and I got out. No kiss.

What to do? Should I stay in with Jacqueline and hate
it and start the slow motor of hating her? Should I make
an excuse and go out? Should I tell the truth and go out?
I can't have it all my own way, relationships are about
compromise. Give and take. Maybe I don't want to stay
in but she wants me to stay in. I should be glad to do
that. It will make us stronger and sweeter. These were
my thoughts as she slept beside me and if she had any
fears she did not reveal them in those night-time hours.
I looked at her lying trustfully in the spot where she had
lain for so many nights. Could this bed be treacherous?

By morning I was bad tempered and exhausted. Jacqueline, ever cheerful, got into her mini and went to her
mother's. At noon she rang to ask me over. Her mother
wasn't well and she wanted to spend the night with her.

'Jacqueline,' I said. 'Stay the night. We'll see each
other tomorrow.'

I felt reprieved and virtuous. Now I could sit in my
own flat by myself and be pragmatic. Sometimes the best
company is your own.

During the interval of *The Marriage of Figaro* I realised
how often other people looked at Louise. On every side
we were battered by sequins, dazed with gold. The wom-
en wore their jewellery like medals. A husband here, a
divorce there, they were a palimpsest of love-affairs. The
chokers, the brooch, the rings, the tiara, the studded watch
that couldn't possibly tell the time to anyone without a
magnifying glass. The bracelets, the ankle-chains, the veil
hung with seed pearls and the earrings that far outnum-

bered the ears. All these jewels were escorted by amply cut grey suits and dashingly spotted ties. The ties twitched when Louise walked by and the suits pulled themselves in a little. The jewels glinted their own warning at Louise's bare throat. She wore a simple dress of moss green silk, a pair of jade earrings, and a wedding ring. 'Never take your eyes from that ring,' I told myself. 'Whenever you think you are falling remember that ring is molten hot and will burn you through and through.'

'What are you looking at?' said Louise.

'You bloody idiot,' said my friend. 'Another married woman.'

Louise and I were talking about Elgin.

'He was born an Orthodox Jew,' she said. 'He feels put upon and superior at the same time.'

Elgin's mother and father still lived in a 1930s semi in Stamford Hill. They had squatted it during the war and made a deal with the Cockney family who eventually came home to find the locks changed and a sign on the parlour door saying SABBATH. KEEP OUT. That was Friday night 1946. On Saturday night 1946 Arnold and Betty Small came face to face with Esau and Sarah Rosenthal. Money changed hands, or to be more precise, a certain amount of gold, and the Smalls went on to bigger things. The Rosenthals opened a chemist shop and refused to serve any Liberal or Reformed Jews.

'We are God's chosen people,' they said, meaning themselves.

From such humble, arrogant beginnings, Elgin was born. They had intended to call him Samuel but, while she was pregnant, Sarah visited the British Museum and, unmoved by the Mummies, came at last to the glory that was Greece. This need not have affected the destiny of her son but Sarah developed serious complications during her fourteen-hour labour and it seemed that she would die. Sweating and delirious, her head twisting from side to side, she could only repeat over and over again the single word ELGIN. Esau, drawn and down at heel, twisting his prayer shawl beneath his black coat, had a superstitious side. If that were his wife's last word then surely it should mean something, become something. And so the word was made flesh. Samuel became Elgin and Sarah did not die. She lived to produce thousands of gallons of chicken soup and whenever she ladled it into the bowl she said, 'Elgin, Jehovah spared me to serve you.'

And so Elgin grew up thinking that the world ought to serve him and hating the dark counter in his father's little shop and hating being set apart from the other boys but wanting it more than anything.

'You're nothing, you're dust,' said Esau. 'Raise yourself up and be a man.'

Elgin won a scholarship to an Independent school. He was small, narrow-chested, short-sighted and ferociously clever. Unfortunately his religion excluded him from Saturday games and whilst he managed to avoid persecution he courted isolation. He knew he was better than those square-shouldered upright beauty queens whose good looks and easy manners commanded affection and respect. Besides, they were all queer, and Elgin had seen them grappling one another, mouths open, cocks hard. No-one tried to touch him.

He fell in love with Louise when she beat him in single combat at the Debating Society finals. Her school was only a mile away from his and he had to walk past it on the way home. He took to walking past it at just the time when Louise was leaving. He was gentle with her, he tried hard, he didn't show off, he wasn't sarcastic. She had only been in England for a year and it was cold. They were both refugees and they found comfort in each other. Then Elgin went to Cambridge, choosing a college outstanding for its sporting prowess. Louise, arriving a year later, had just begun to suspect him of being a masochist. This was confirmed when he lay on his single bed, legs apart, and begged her to scaffold his penis with bulldog clips.

'I can take it,' he said. 'I'm going to be a doctor.'

Meanwhile, at home in Stamford Hill, Esau and Sarah, locked in prayer through the twenty-four hours of the Sabbath, wondered what would happen to their boy who had fallen into the clutches of a flame-haired temptress.

'She'll ruin him,' said Esau, 'he's doomed. We're all doomed.'

'My boy, my boy,' said Sarah. 'And only five feet seven.'

They didn't attend the wedding held in a Registry Office in Cambridge. How could they when Elgin had arranged it for a Saturday? There was Louise in an ivory silk flapper dress with a silver headband. Her best friend Janet holding a camera and the rings. Elgin's best friend whose name he couldn't remember. Elgin, in a hired morning suit just a size too tight.

'You see,' said Louise, 'I knew he was safe, that I could control him, that I would be the one in charge.'

'And what about him, what did he think?'

'He knew I was beautiful, that I was a prize. He wanted something showy but not vulgar. He wanted to go up to the world and say, "Look what I've got." '

I thought about Elgin. He was very eminent, very dull, very rich. Louise charmed everyone. She brought him attention, contacts, she cooked, she decorated, she was clever and above all she was beautiful. Elgin was awkward and he didn't fit. There was a certain amount of racism in the way he was treated. His colleagues were mostly those young men he had been taught with and inwardly despised. He knew other Jews of course, but in his profession they were all comfortable, cultured, liberal. They weren't Orthodox from Stamford Hill with nothing but a squatted semi between themselves and the gas chamber. Elgin never talked about his past, and gradually, with Louise beside him, it became irrelevant. He too became comfortable and cultivated and liberal. He went to the opera and he bought antiques. He made jokes about Frummers and matzos and even lost his accent. When Louise encouraged him to get in touch with his parents he sent them a Christmas card.

'It's her,' said Esau behind the dark counter. 'A curse on women since the sin of Eve.'

And Sarah, polishing, sorting, mending, serving, felt the curse and lost herself a little more.

'Hello Elgin,' I said as he came into the kitchen in his navy blue corduroys (size M) and his off-duty Viyella shirt (size S). He leaned against the stove and fired a staccato of questions at me. That was his preferred method of conversation; it meant he didn't have to expose himself.

Louise was chopping vegetables. 'Elgin's going away next week,' she said, cutting through his flow as deftly as he would a windpipe.

'That's right, that's right,' he said cheerfully. 'Got a paper to give in Washington. Ever been to Washington?'

Tuesday the twelfth of May 10.40. British Airways flight to Washington cleared for take-off. There's Elgin in Club Class with his glass of champagne and his headphones on listening to Wagner. Bye Bye Elgin.

Tuesday the twelfth of May 1 pm. Knock Knock.
  'Who's there?'
  'Hello Louise.'
  She smiled. 'Just in time for lunch.'

Is food sexy? *Playboy* regularly features stories about asparagus and bananas and leeks and courgettes or being smeared with honey or chocolate chip ice-cream. I once bought some erotic body oil, authentic Pina Colada flavour, and poured it over myself but it made my lover's tongue come out in a rash.

Then there are candle-lit dinners and those leering waistcoated waiters with outsize pepperpots. There are, too, simple picnics on the beach which only work when you're in love because otherwise you couldn't bear the sand in the brie. Context is all, or so I thought, until I started eating with Louise.

When she lifted the soup spoon to her lips how I longed to be that innocent piece of stainless steel. I would gladly have traded the blood in my body for half a pint of vegetable stock. Let me be diced carrot, vermicelli, just so that you will take me in your mouth. I envied the French stick. I watched her break and butter each piece, soak it slowly in her bowl, let it float, grow heavy and fat, sink under the deep red weight and then be resurrected to the glorious pleasure of her teeth.

The potatoes, the celery, the tomatoes, all had been under her hands. When I ate my own soup I strained to taste her skin. She had been here, there must be something of her left. I would find her in the oil and onions, detect her through the garlic. I knew that she spat in the frying pan to determine the readiness of the oil. It's an old trick, every chef does it, or did. And so I knew when I asked her what was in the soup that she had deleted the essential ingredient. I will taste you if only through your cooking.

She split a pear; one of her own pears from the garden. Where she lived had been an orchard once and her particular tree was two hundred and twenty years old. Older than the French Revolution. Old enough to have fed Wordsworth and Napoleon. Who had gone into this garden and plucked the fruit? Did their hearts beat as hard as mine? She offered me half a pear and a piece of Parmesan cheese. Such pears as these have seen the world, that is they have stayed still and the world has seen them. At each bite burst war and passion. History was rolled in the pips and the frog-coloured skin.

She dribbled viscous juices down her chin and before I could help her wiped them away. I eyed the napkin; could I steal it? Already my hand was creeping over the tablecloth like something out of Poe. She touched me and I yelped.

'Did I scratch you?' she said, all concern and remorse.

'No, you electrocuted me.'

She got up and put on the coffee. The English are very good at those gestures.

'Are we going to have an affair?' she said.

She's not English, she's Australian.

'No, no we're not,' I said. 'You're married and I'm with Jacqueline. We're going to be friends.'

She said, 'We're friends already.'

Yes we are and I do like to pass the day with you in serious and inconsequential chatter. I wouldn't mind washing up beside you, dusting beside you, reading the back half of the paper while you read the front. We are friends and I would miss you, do miss you and think of you very often. I don't want to lose this happy space where I have found someone who is smart and easy and who doesn't bother to check her diary when we arrange to meet. All the way home I told myself these things and these things were the solid pavement beneath my feet and the neat clipped hedges and the corner shop and Jacqueline's car. Everything in its place; the lover, the friend, the life, the set. At home the breakfast cups are where we left them and I know, even if I close my eyes, the exact spot of Jacqueline's pyjamas. I used to think that Christ was wrong, impossibly hard, when he said that to imagine committing adultery was just as bad as doing it. But now, standing here in this familiar unviolated space, I have already altered my world and Jacqueline's world for ever. She doesn't know this yet. She doesn't know that there is today a revision of the map. That the territory she thought was hers has been annexed. You never give away your heart; you lend it from time to time. If it were not so how could we take it back without asking?

I welcomed the quiet hours of late afternoon. No-one would disturb me, I could make smoky tea and sit in my usual place and hope that the wisdom of objects would make some difference to me. Here, surrounded by my tables and chairs and books, I would surely see the need to stay in one place. I had been an emotional nomad for too long. Hadn't I come here weak and bruised to put a fence round the space Louise now threatened?

Oh Louise, I'm not telling the truth. You aren't threatening me, I'm threatening myself. My careful well-earned life means nothing. The clock was ticking. I thought, How long before the shouting starts? How long before the tears and accusations and the pain? That specific stone in the stomach pain when you lose something you haven't got round to valuing? Why is the measure of love loss?

This prelude and forethought is not unusual but to admit it is to cut through our one way out; the grand excuse of passion. You had no choice, you were swept away. Forces took you and possessed you and you did it but now that's all in the past, you can't understand etc etc. You want to start again etc etc. Forgive me. In the late twentieth century we still look to ancient daemons to explain our commonest action. Adultery is very common. It has no rarity value and yet at an individual level it is explained away again and again as a UFO. I can't lie to myself in quite that way any more. I always did but not now. I know exactly what's happening and I know too that I am jumping out of this plane of my own free will. No, I don't have a parachute, but worse, neither does Jacqueline. When you go you take one with you.

I cut a slice of fruit bread. If in doubt eat. I can understand why for some people the best social worker is the fridge. My usual confessional is a straight Macallan but not before 5 o'clock. Perhaps that's why I try and have my crises in the evening. Well, here I am at half past four with fruit bread and a cup of tea and instead of taking hold of myself I can only think of taking hold of Louise. It's the food that's doing it. There could not be a more unromantic moment than this and yet the yeasty smell of raisins and rye is exciting me more than any *Playboy* banana. It's only a matter of time. Is it nobler to struggle for a week before flying out the door or should I go and get my toothbrush now? I am drowning in inevitability.

I phoned a friend whose advice was to play the sailor and run a wife in every port. If I told Jacqueline I'd ruin everything and for what? If I told Jacqueline I'd hurt her beyond healing and did I have that right? Probably I had nothing more than dog-fever for two weeks and I could get it out of my system and come home to my kennel.

Good sense. Common sense. Good dog.

What does it say in the tea-leaves? Nothing but a capital L.

When Jacqueline came home I kissed her and said, 'I wish you didn't smell of the Zoo.'

She looked surprised. 'I can't help it. Zoos are smelly places.'

She went immediately to run a bath. I gave her a drink thinking how I disliked her clothes and the way she switched on the radio as soon as she got in.

Grimly I began to prepare our dinner. What would we do this evening? I felt like a bandit who hides a gun in his mouth. If I spoke I would reveal everything. Better not to speak. Eat, smile, make space for Jacqueline. Surely that was right?

The phone rang. I skidded to get it, closing the bedroom door behind me.

It was Louise.

'Come over tomorrow,' she said. 'There's something I want to tell you.'

'Louise, if it's to do with today, I can't . . . you see, I've decided I can't. That is I couldn't because, well what if, you know . . . '

The phone clicked and went dead. I stared at it the way Lauren Bacall does in those films with Humphrey Bogart. What I need now is a car with a running board and a pair of fog lights. I could be with you in ten minutes Louise. The trouble is that all I've got is a Mini belonging to my girlfriend.

We were eating our spaghetti. I thought, As long as I don't say her name I'll be all right. I started a game with myself, counting out on the cynical clock face the extent of my success. What am I? I feel like a kid in the examination room faced with a paper I can't complete. Let the clock go faster. Let me get out of here. At 9 o'clock I told Jacqueline I was exhausted. She reached over and took my hand. I felt nothing. And then there we were in our pyjamas side by side and my lips were sealed and my cheeks must have been swelling out like a gerbil's because my mouth was full of Louise.

I don't have to tell you where I went the next day.

During the night I had a lurid dream about an ex-girlfriend of mine who had been heavily into papier-mâché. It had started as a hobby; and who shall object to a few buckets of flour and water and a roll of chicken wire? I'm a liberal and I believe in free expression. I went to her house one day and poking out of the letter-box just at crotch level was the head of a yellow and green serpent. Not a real one but livid enough with a red tongue and silver foil teeth. I hesitated to ring the bell. Hesitated because to reach the bell meant pushing my private parts right into the head of the snake. I held a little dialogue with myself.

ME: Don't be silly. It's a joke.

I: What do you mean it's a joke? It's lethal.

ME: Those teeth aren't real.

I: They don't have to be real to be painful.

ME: What will she think of you if you stand here all night?

I: What does she think of me anyway? What kind of a girl aims a snake at your genitals?

ME: A fun-loving girl.

I: Ha Ha.

The door flew open and Amy stood on the mat. She was wearing a kaftan and a long string of beads. 'It won't hurt you,' she said. 'It's for the postman. He's been bothering me.'

'I don't think it's going to frighten him,' I said. 'It's only a toy snake. It didn't frighten me.'

'You've nothing to be frightened of,' she said. 'It's got a rat-trap in the jaw.' She disappeared inside while I stood hovering on the step holding my bottle of Beaujolais Nouveau. She returned with a leek and shoved it in the snake's mouth. There was a terrible clatter and the bottom half of the leek fell limply on to the mat. 'Bring it in with you will you?' she said. 'We're eating it later.'

I awoke sweating and chilled. Jacqueline slept peacefully beside me, the light was leaking through the old curtains. Muffled in my dressing gown I went into the garden, glad of the wetness sudden beneath my feet. The air was clean with a hint of warmth and the sky had pink clawmarks pulled through it. There was an urban pleasure in knowing that I was the only one breathing the air. The relentless in-out-in-out of millions of lungs depresses me. There are too many of us on this planet and it's beginning to show. My neighbour's blinds were down. What were their dreams and nightmares? How different it would be to see them now, slack in the jaw, bodies open. We might be able to say something truthful to one another instead of the usual rolled-up Goodmornings.

I went to look at my sunflowers, growing steadily, sure that the sun would be there for them, fulfilling themselves in the proper way at the proper time. Very few people ever manage what nature manages without effort and mostly without fail. We don't know who we are or how to function, much less how to bloom. Blind nature. Homo sapiens. Who's kidding whom?

So what am I going to do? I asked Robin on the wall. Robins are very faithful creatures who mate with the same mate year by year. I love the brave red shield on their breast and the determined way they follow the spade in search of worms. There am I doing all the digging and there's little Robin making off with the worm. Homo sapiens. Blind Nature.

I don't feel wise. Why is it that human beings are allowed to grow up without the necessary apparatus to make sound ethical decisions?

The facts of my case are not unusual:

1   I have fallen in love with a woman who is married.
2   She has fallen in love with me.
3   I am committed to someone else.
4   How shall I know whether Louise is what I must do or must avoid?

The church could tell me, my friends have tried to help me, I could take the stoic course and run from temptation or I could put up sail and tack into this gathering wind.

For the first time in my life, I want to do the right

thing more than I want to get my own way. I suppose
I owe that to Bathsheba . . .

I remember her visiting my house soon after she had
returned from a six-week trip to South Africa. Before
she had gone, I had given her an ultimatum: Him or me.
Her eyes, which very often filled with tears of self-pity,
had reproached me for yet another lover's half-nelson. I
forced her to it and of course she made the decision for
him. All right. Six weeks. I felt like the girl in the story
of Rumpelstiltskin who is given a cellar full of straw to
weave into gold by the following morning. All I had ever
got from Bathsheba were bales of straw but when she
was with me I believed that they were promises carved
in precious stone. So I had to face up to the waste and
the mess and I worked hard to sweep the chaff away.
Then she came in, unrepentant, her memory gone as
ever, wondering why I hadn't returned her trunk calls
or written poste restante.

'I meant what I said.'

She sat in silence for about fifteen minutes while I
glued the legs back on a kitchen chair. Then she asked
me if I was seeing anybody else. I said I was, briefly,
vaguely, hopefully.

She nodded and turned to go. When she got to the
door she said, 'I intended to tell you before we left but I
forgot.'

I looked at her, sudden and sharp. I hated that 'we'.

'Yes,' she went on, 'Uriah got NSU from a woman
he slept with in New York. He slept with her to punish
me of course. But he didn't tell me and the doctor thinks I
have it too. I've been taking the antibiotics so it's probably
all right. That is, you're probably all right. You ought to
check though.'

I came at her with the leg of the chair. I wanted to run it straight across her perfectly made-up face.

'You shit.'

'Don't say that.'

'You told me you weren't having sex with him any more.'

'I thought it was unfair. I didn't want to shatter what little sexual confidence he might have left.'

'I suppose that's why you've never bothered to tell him that he doesn't know how to make you come.'

She didn't answer. She was crying now. It was like blood in the water to me. I circled her.

'How long is it you've been married? The perfect public marriage. Ten years, twelve? And you don't ask him to put his head between your legs because you think he'll find it distasteful. Let's hear it for sexual confidence.'

'Stop it,' she said, pushing me away. 'I have to go home.'

'It must be seven o'clock. That's your home-time isn't it? That's why you used to leave the practice early so that you could get a quick fuck for an hour and a half and then smooth yourself down to say, "Hello darling," and cook dinner.'

'You let me come,' she said.

'Yes, I did, when you were bleeding, when you were sick, again and again I made you come.'

'I didn't mean that. I meant we did it together. You wanted me there.'

'I wanted you everywhere and the pathetic thing is I still do.'

She looked at me. 'Drive me home will you?'

I still remember that night with shame and rage. I didn't

≈ 45 ≈

drive her home. I walked with her through the dark lanes to her house hearing the swish of her trenchcoat and the rub of her briefcase against her calf. Like Dirk Bogarde she prided herself on her profile and it was lit to suitable effect under the dull streetlights. I left her where I knew she'd be safe and listened to the click of her heels dying away. After a few seconds they stopped. I was familiar with this; she was checking her hair and her face, dusting me from coat and loins. The gate squeaked and closed metal on metal. They were inside now, four-square, everything shared, even the disease.

As I walked home, breathing deeply, knowing that I was shaking and not knowing how to stop it, I thought, I'm as guilty as her. Hadn't I let it happen, colluded with the deceit and let all my pride be burnt away? I was nothing, a weak piece of shit, I deserved Bathsheba. Self-respect. They're supposed to teach you that in the Army. Perhaps I should enlist. Would it recommend me though, to write Broken Heart under Personal Interests?

At the Clap Clinic the following day, I looked at my fellow sufferers. Shifty Jack-the-lads, fat businessmen in suits cut to hide the bulge. A few women, tarts yes, and other women too. Women with eyes full of pain and fear. What was this place and why had nobody told them? 'Who gave it to you love?' I wanted to say to one middle-aged woman in a floral print. She kept staring at the posters about gonorrhoea and then trying to concentrate on her copy of *Country Life*. 'Divorce him,' I wanted to say. 'You think this is the first time?' Her name was called and she disappeared into a bleak white room. This place is like the ante-chamber to Judgement Day. A pot of stale Cona coffee, a few scruffy leatherette benches, plastic flowers in a plastic vase and all over the walls, top to bottom, posters for every genital wart and discoloured emission. It's impressive what a few inches of flesh can catch.

Ah, Bathsheba, it's not the same as your elegant surgery is it? There your private patients can have their teeth removed to Vivaldi and enjoy twenty minutes' rest on a reclining sofa. Your flowers are delivered fresh every day and you serve only the most aromatic herbal teas. Against your white coat, their heads on your breast, no-one fears the needle and syringe. I came to you for a crown and you offered me a kingdom. Unfortunately I could only take possession between five and seven, weekdays, and the odd weekend when he was away playing football.

My name was called.

'Have I got it?'

The nurse looked at me the way you do a flat tyre and said, 'No.'

Then she started filling out a form and told me to come back in three months.

'What for?'

'Sexually transmitted diseases are not normally an isolated problem. If your habits are such that you have caught it once it's likely that you will catch it again.' She paused. 'We are creatures of habit.'

'I haven't caught it, any of it.'

She opened the door. 'Three months will be sufficient.'

Sufficient for what? I walked down the corridor past SURGERY and MOTHER AND BABY and OUTPATIENTS THIS WAY. It's a feature of the Clap Clinic that it's situated well out of the way of proper deserving patients. Its labyrinthian cunning means that the user will have to ask at least five times how to get there. Although I lowered my voice, particularly in deference to MOTHER AND BABY, I was returned no such courtesy. 'Venereal Disease? Down the end turn right turn left straight on through the gates past the lift up the stairs down the corridor round the corner, through the swing doors and there you are,' yelled the male nurse, carefully stopping his trolley-load of dirty sheets on my foot . . . 'You did say VENEREAL?'

Yes I did, and I said it again to the junior doctor rakishly swinging his stethoscope at the OUTPATIENTS. 'Clap Clinic? No problem, you're not more than five minutes away by wheelchair.' He pealed with laughter like a posse of ice-cream vans and pointed in the direction of the incinerator chute. 'That's the quickest way. Good luck.'

Maybe it's my face. Maybe I look like a doormat today. I feel like one.

On the way out I bought myself a large bunch of flowers.

'Visiting someone?' said the girl, her voice going up at the corners like a hospital sandwich. She was bored to death, having to be nice, jammed behind the ferns, her right hand dripping with green water.

'Yes, myself. I want to find out how I am.'

She raised her eyebrows and squeaked, 'You all right?'

'I shall be,' I said, throwing her a carnation.

At home, I put the flowers in a vase, changed the sheets and got into bed. 'What did Bathsheba ever give me but a perfect set of teeth?'

'All the better to eat you with,' said the Wolf.

I got a can of spray paint and wrote SELF-RESPECT over the door.

Let Cupid try and get past that one.

Louise was eating breakfast when I arrived. She was wearing a red and green guardsman stripe dressing gown gloriously too large. Her hair was down, warming her neck and shoulders, falling forward on to the table-cloth in wires of light. There was a dangerously electrical quality about Louise. I worried that the steady flame she offered might be fed by a current far more volatile. Superficially she seemed serene, but beneath her control was a crackling power of the kind that makes me nervous when I pass pylons. She was more of a Victorian heroine than a modern woman. A heroine from a Gothic novel, mistress of her house, yet capable of setting fire to it and fleeing in the night with one bag. I always expected her to wear her keys at her waist. She was compressed, stoked down, a volcano dormant but not dead. It did occur to me that if Louise were a volcano then I might be Pompeii.

I didn't go in straight away, I stood lurking outside with my collar turned up, hiding to get a better view. I thought, If she calls the police, it's only what I deserve. But she wouldn't call the police, she'd take her pearl-handled revolver from the glass decanter and shoot me through the heart. At the post-mortem they'll find an enlarged heart and no guts.

The white table-cloth, the brown teapot. The chrome toast-rack and the silver-bladed knives. Ordinary things. Look how she picks them up and puts them down, wipes her hands briskly on the edge of the table-cloth; she wouldn't do that in company. She's finished her egg, I can see the top jagged on the plate, a bit of butter that she pops into her mouth from the end of her knife. Now she's gone for a bath and the kitchen's empty. Silly kitchen without Louise.

It was easy for me to get in, the door was unlocked. I felt like a thief with a bagful of stolen glances. It's odd being in someone else's room when they're not there.

Especially when you love them. Every object carries a different significance. Why did she buy that? What does she especially like? Why does she sit in this chair and not that one? The room becomes a code that you have only a few minutes to crack. When she returns, she will command your attention, and besides it's rude to stare. And yet I want to pull out the drawers and run my fingers under the dusty rims of the pictures. In the waste basket perhaps, in the larder, I will find a clue to you, I will be able to unravel you, pull you between my fingers and stretch out each thread to know the measure of you. The compulsion to steal something is ridiculous, intense. I don't want one of your EPNS spoons, charming though they are, with a tiny Edwardian boot on the handle. Why then have I put it in my pocket? 'Take it out at once,' says the Headmistress who keeps an eye on my conduct. I managed to force it back into the drawer, although for a teaspoon it put up a lot of resistance. I sat down and tried to concentrate myself. Right in my eyeline was the laundry basket. Not the laundry basket . . . please.

I have never been a knicker-sniffer. I don't want to lard my inner pockets with used underwear. I know people who do and I sympathise. It's a dicey business going into a tense boardroom with a large white handkerchief on one side of the suit and a slender pair of knickers on the other. How can you be absolutely sure you remember which is where? I was hypnotised by the laundry basket like an out-of-work snake charmer.

I had just got to my feet when Louise strode through the door, her hair piled up on her head and pinned with a tortoiseshell bar. I could smell the steam on her from the bath and the scent of a rough woody soap. She held out her arms, her face softening with love, I took her two hands to my mouth and kissed each slowly so that I could memorise the shape of her knuckles. I didn't only want Louise's flesh, I wanted her bones, her blood, her tissues, the sinews that bound her together. I would have held her to me though time had stripped away the tones and textures of her skin. I could have held her for a thousand years until the skeleton itself rubbed away to dust. What are you that makes me feel thus? Who are you for whom time has no meaning?

In the heat of her hands I thought, This is the campfire that mocks the sun. This place will warm me, feed me and care for me. I will hold on to this pulse against other rhythms. The world will come and go in the tide of a day but here is her hand with my future in its palm.

She said, 'Come upstairs.'

We climbed one behind the other past the landing on the first floor, the studio on the second, up where the stairs narrowed and the rooms were smaller. It seemed that the house would not end, that the stairs in their twisting shape took us higher and out of the house altogether into an attic in a tower where birds beat against the windows and the sky was an offering. There was a small bed with a patchwork quilt. The floor sheered to one side, one board prised up like a wound. The walls, bumpy and distempered, were breathing. I could feel them moving under my touch. They were damp, slightly. The light, channelled by the thin air, heated the panes of glass too hot to open. We were magnified in this high wild room. You and I could reach the ceiling and the floor and every side of our loving cell. You kissed me and I tasted the relish of your skin.

What then? That you, so recently dressed, lost your clothes in an unconscious pile and I found you wore a petticoat. Louise, your nakedness was too complete for me, who had not learned the extent of your fingers. How could I cover this land? Did Columbus feel like this on sighting the Americas? I had no dreams to possess you but I wanted you to possess me.

It was a long time later that I heard the noise of schoolchildren on their way home. Their voices, high-pitched and eager, carried up past the sedater rooms and came at last, distorted, to our House of Fame. Perhaps we were in the roof of the world, where Chaucer had been with his eagle. Perhaps the rush and press of life ended here, the voices collecting in the rafters, repeating themselves into redundancy. Energy cannot be lost only transformed; where do the words go?

'Louise, I love you.'

Very gently, she put her hand over my mouth and shook her head. 'Don't say that now. Don't say it yet. You might not mean it.'

I was protesting with a stream of superlatives, beginning to sound like an advertising hack. Naturally this model had to be the best the most important, the wonderful even the incomparable. Nouns have no worth these days unless they bank with a couple of Highstreet adjectives. The more I underlined it the hollower it sounded. Louise said nothing and eventually I shut up.

'When I said you might not mean it, I meant it might not be possible for you to mean it.'

'I'm not married.'

'You think that makes you free?'

'It makes me freer.'

'It also makes it easier for you to change your mind. I don't doubt that you would leave Jacqueline. But would you stay with me?'

'I love you.'

'You've loved other people but you still left them.'

'It's not that simple.'

'I don't want to be another scalp on your pole.'

'You started this, Louise.'

'I acknowledged it. We both started it.'

What was all this about? We had made love once. We had known each other as friends for a couple of months and yet she was challenging my suitability as a long-term candidate? I said as much.

'So you admit that I am just a scalp?'

I was angry and bewildered. 'Louise, I don't know what you are. I've turned myself inside out to try and avoid what happened today. You affect me in ways I can't quantify or contain. All I can measure is the effect, and the effect is that I am out of control.'

'So you try and regain control by telling me you love me. That's a territory you know, isn't it? That's romance and courtship and whirlwind.'

'I don't want control.'

'I don't believe you.'

No and you're right not to believe me. If in doubt be sincere. That's a pretty little trick of mine. I got up and reached for my shirt. It was under her petticoat. I picked up the petticoat instead.

'May I have this?'

'Trophy hunting?'

Her eyes were full of tears. I had hurt her. I regretted telling her those stories about my girlfriends. I had wanted to make her laugh and she had laughed at the time. Now I had strewn our path with barbs. She didn't trust me. As a friend I had been amusing. As a lover I was lethal. I could see that. I wouldn't want to have much to do with me. I knelt on the floor and clasped her legs against my chest.

'Tell me what you want and I'll do it.'

She stroked my hair. 'I want you to come to me without a past. Those lines you've learned, forget them. Forget that you've been here before in other bedrooms in other places. Come to me new. Never say you love me until that day when you have proved it.'

'How shall I prove it?'

'I can't tell you what to do.'

The maze. Find your own way through and you shall win your heart's desire. Fail and you will wander for ever in these unforgiving walls. Is that the test? I told you that Louise had more than a notion of the Gothic about her. She seemed determined that I should win her from the tangle of my own past. In her attic room was a print of the Burne-Jones picture titled *Love and the Pilgrim*. An angel in clean garments leads by the hand a traveller footsore and weary. The traveller is in black and her cloak is still caught by the dense thicket of thorns from which they have both emerged. Would Louise lead me so? Did I want to be led? She was right, I hadn't thought about the hugeness of it all. I had some excuse; I was thinking about Jacqueline.

It was raining when I left Louise's house and caught a bus to the Zoo. The bus was full of women and children. Tired busy women placating cross excitable kids. One child had forced her brother's head into his satchel, scattering schoolbooks over the rubber floor, enraging her pretty young mother to the point of murder. Why is none of this work included in the Gross National Product? 'Because we don't know how to quantify it,' say the economists. They should try catching a bus.

I got off at the main entrance to the Animal House. The boy in the booth was bored and alone. He had his feet propped on the turnstile, the wet wind pushing through his window and spatting his micro TV. He didn't look at me as I leaned for shelter against a perspex elephant.

'Zoo's shuttin' in ten,' he said mysteriously. 'No admin after five pm.'

A secretary's dream; 'No admin after five pm.' That amused me for two seconds and then I saw Jacqueline coming towards the gate, her beret pulled against the drizzle. She had a carrier bag full of food, leeks prodding through the sides.

'Nite luv,' said the boy without moving his lips.

She hadn't seen me. I wanted to hide behind the perspex elephant, jump out at her and say, 'Let's go for dinner.'

I am often beset by such romantic follies. I use them as ways out of real situations. Who the hell wants to go for dinner at 5.30 pm? Who wants to have a sexy walk in the rain alongside thousands of home-time commuters, all like you, carrying a shopping bag full of food?

'Stick to it,' I told myself. 'Go on.'

'Jacqueline.' (I sound like someone from the CID.)

She turned up her face, smiles and pleasure, handed me the bag and wrapped herself in the coat. She started walking towards her car, telling me about her day, there was a wallaby that had needed counselling, did I know that the Zoo used them in animal experiments? The Zoo decapitated them alive. It was in the interests of science.

'But not in the interests of wallabies?'

'No,' she said. 'And why should they suffer? You wouldn't chop my head off, would you?'

I looked at her appalled. She was joking but it didn't feel like a joke.

'Let's go and get some coffee and a bit of cake.' I took her arm and we walked away from the carpark towards a homely tea-shoppe that normally served the outflow of the Zoo. It was pleasant when the visitors weren't there and they weren't there on that day. The animals must pray for rain.

'You don't usually pick me up from work,' she said.

'No.'

'Is there something to celebrate?'

'No.'

Condensation ran down the windows. Nothing was clear any more.

'Is it about Louise?'

I nodded, twisting the cake fork between my fingers, pushing my knees against the underside of the dolls' house table. Nothing was in proportion. My voice seemed too loud, Jacqueline too small, the woman serving dough-nuts with mechanical efficiency parked her bosom on the glass counter and threatened to shatter it with mammary power. How she would skittle the chocolate eclairs and with a single plop drown her unwary customers in mock cream. My mother always said I'd come to a sticky end.

'Are you seeing her?' Jacqueline's timid voice.

Irritation from gut to gullet. I wanted to snarl like the dog I am.

'Of course I'm seeing her. I see her face on every hoarding, on the coins in my pocket. I see her when I look at you. I see her when I don't look at you.'

I didn't say any of that, I mumbled something about yes as usual but things had changed. THINGS HAD CHANGED, what an arsehole comment, I had changed things. Things don't change, they're not like the seasons moving on a diurnal round. People change things. There are victims of change but not victims of things. Why do I collude in this mis-use of language? I can't make it easier for Jacqueline however I put it. I can make it a bit easier for me and I suppose that's what I'm doing.

She said, 'I thought you'd changed.'

'I have, that's the problem, isn't it?'

'I thought you'd already changed. You told me you wouldn't do this again. You told me you wanted a different life. It's easy to hurt me.'

What she says is true. I did think I could leave with the morning paper and come home for the 6 o'clock news. I hadn't lied to Jacqueline but it seemed I had been lying to myself.

'I'm not running around again, Jacqueline.'

'What *are* you doing then?'

Good point. Would that I had the overseeing spirit to interpret my actions in plain English. I would like to come to you with all the confidence of a computer programmer, sure that we could find the answers if only we asked the proper questions. Why aren't I going according to plan? How stupid it sounds to say I don't know and shrug and behave like every other idiot who's fallen in love and can't explain it. I've had a lot of practice, I should be able to explain it. The only word I can think of is Louise.

Jacqueline, exposed under tea-shoppe neon, wraps her hands around her cup for comfort but gets burned. She spills into her saucer and, while mopping at it with the inadequate serviette, knocks her cake on to the floor. Silently but with eagle eye, the Bosom bends to clear it up. She's seen it all before, it doesn't interest her except that she wants to close in a quarter of an hour. She retreats behind her counter and switches on the radio.

Jacqueline wiped her glasses.

'What are you going to do?'

'It's for us to decide that. It's a joint decision.'

'You mean we'll talk about it and you'll do what you want anyway.'

'I don't know what I want.'

She nodded and got up to leave. By the time I had found the change to pay our host Jacqueline was somewhere down the street, going for her car I thought.

I ran to catch up with her but when I got to the Zoo carpark it was locked. I caught hold of the diamond-shaped tennis netting and vainly shook the smug padlock. A wet May night, more like February than sweet spring, it should have been soft and light but the light was soaked up by a row of weary streetlamps reflecting the rain. Jacqueline's Mini stood alone in a corner of the bleak paddock. Ridiculous this waste sad time.

I walked across to a small park and sat on a damp bench under a dripping willow. I was wearing baggy shorts which in such weather looked like a recruitment campaign for the Boy Scouts. But I'm not a Boy Scout and never was. I envy them; they know exactly what makes a Good Deed.

Opposite me, the relaxed smart houses built on the park showed yellow at one window, black at another. A figure pulled the curtains, someone opened the front door, I could hear music for a moment. What sane sensible lives. Did those people lie awake at night hiding their hearts while giving their bodies? Did the woman at the window quietly despair as the clock pushed her closer to bed-time? Does she love her husband? Desire him? When he sees his wife unlace herself what does he feel? In a different house is there someone he longs for the way he used to long for her?

At the fairground there used to be a penny slot-machine called 'What the Butler Saw'. You jammed your eyes against a padded viewfinder, put in the coin and at once a troupe of dancing girls started tossing their skirts and winking. Gradually they cast off most of their clothes, but if you wanted the coup de grace you had to get in another coin before the butler's white hand drew a discreet blind. The pleasure of it, apart from the obvious, was depth simulation. It was intended to give the feel of a toff at the music hall, in the best seat of course. You could see rows of velvet seats and a rake of Brylcreemed hair. It was delicious because it was puerile and naughty. I always felt guilty but it was a hot thrill of guilt not the dreadful weight of sin. Those days made me a voyeur, though of a modest kind. I like to pass by bare windows and get a sighting of the life within.

No silent films were shot in colour but the pictures through a window are that. Everything moves in curious clockwork animation. Why is that man throwing up his arms? The girl's hands move soundlessly over the piano. Only half an inch of glass separates me from the silent world where I do not exist. They don't know I'm here but I have begun to be as intimate with them as any member of the family. More so, since as their lips move with goldfish bowl pouts, I am the scriptwriter and I can put words in their mouths. I had a girlfriend once, we used to play that game, going round the posh houses when we were down at heel making up stories about the lamplit well-to-do.

Her name was Catherine, she wanted to be a writer. She said it was good exercise for her imagination to invent little scenarios for the unsuspecting. I don't want to be a writer but I didn't mind carrying her pad. It did occur to me, those dark nights, that movies are a terrible sham. In real life, left to their own devices, especially after 7 o'clock, human beings hardly move at all. Sometimes I panicked and told Catherine we'd have to call the ambulance.

'No-one can sit still for that long,' I said. 'She must be dead. Look at her, rigor mortis has set in, not so much as a squint.'

Then we'd go to an arthouse showing of Chabrol or Renoir and the entire cast spent the whole picture running in and out of bedrooms and shooting at one another and getting divorced. I was exhausted. The French crack on about being an intellectual resource but for a nation of thinkers they do run around a lot. Thinking is supposed to be a sedentary occupation. They pack more action into their arty films than the Americans manage in a dozen Clint Eastwoods. *Jules et Jim* is an action movie.

We were so happy those wet carefree nights. I felt we were like Dr Watson and Sherlock Holmes. I knew my place. And then Catherine said she was leaving. She didn't want to do it but she felt that a writer doesn't make a good companion. 'It's only a matter of time', she said, 'before I become an alcoholic and forget how to cook.'

I suggested we wait and try and ride it out. She shook her head sadly and patted me. 'Get a dog.'

Naturally I was devastated. I enjoyed our wandering nights together, the brief stop at the fish shop, falling into the same bed at dawn.

'Is there anything I can do for you before you go?' I asked.

'Yes,' she said. 'Do you know why Henry Miller said "I write with my prick"?'

'Because he did. When he died they found nothing between his legs but a ball-point pen.'

'You're making it up,' she said.

Am I?

I was sitting on the bench smiling soaked to the skin. I wasn't happy but the power of memory is such that it can lift reality for a time. Or is memory the more real place? I stood up and wrung out the legs of my shorts. It was dark, the park belonged to other people after dark and I didn't belong to them. Best to go home and find Jacqueline.

When I got to my flat the door was locked. I tried to get in but the chain was across the door. I shouted and banged. At last the letter-box flipped open and a note slid out. It said GO AWAY. I found a pen and wrote on the backside. IT'S MY FLAT. As I feared there was no response. For the second time that day I ended up at Louise's.

'We're going to sleep in a different bed tonight,' she said as she filled the bathroom with clouds of steam and incense oils. 'I'm going to warm the room and you're going to lie in the tub and drink this cocoa. All right Christopher Robin?'

Yes, with or without a blue hood. How tender this is and how unlikely. I don't believe any of it. Jacqueline must have known I'd have to come here. Why would she do that? They're not in it together are they, to punish me? Perhaps I've died and this is Judgement Day. Judgement or not I can't go back to Jacqueline. Whatever happens here, and I held out no great hopes, I knew that I'd split myself from her in ways that were too profound to heal. In the park in the rain I had recognised one thing at least; that Louise was the woman I wanted even if I couldn't have her. Jacqueline I had to admit had never been wanted, simply she had had roughly the right shape to fit for a while.

Molecular docking is a serious challenge for bio-chemists. There are many ways to fit molecules together but only a few juxtapositions that bring them close enough to bond. On a molecular level success may mean discovering what synthetic structure, what chemical, will form a union with, say, the protein shape on a tumour cell. If you make this high-risk jigsaw work you may have found a cure for carcinoma. But molecules and the human beings they are a part of exist in a universe of possibility. We touch one another, bond and break, drift away on force-fields we don't understand. Docking here inside Louise may heal a damaged heart, on the other hand it may be an expensively ruinous experiment.

I put on the rough towelling robe Louise had left for me. I hoped it wasn't Elgin's. There used to be a scam in the undertaking trade whereby any man sent to the Chapel of Rest in a good suit of clothes had the lot tried on by the embalmer and his boys while he, the deceased, was made ready for the grave. Whoever the clothes best fitted put a shilling on them; that is, the shilling went in the Poor Box and the clothes went off the dead man's back. Obviously he was allowed to wear them while ritual viewing took place but as soon as it was time for the lid to be screwed down, one of the lads whipped them off and covered the unfortunate in a cheap winding sheet. If I was going to stab Elgin in the back I didn't want to do it in his dressing gown.

'That's mine,' said Louise as I came upstairs. 'Don't worry.'

'How did you know?'

'Do you remember when you and I were caught in that terrible shower on the way to your flat? Jacqueline insisted that I undress and she gave me her dressing gown to wear. It was very kind but I longed to be in yours. It was your smell I was after.'

'Wasn't I in mine?'

'Yes. All the more tempting.'

She had lit a fire in the room with the bed she'd called a Lady's Occasional. Most people don't have open fires any more; Louise had no central heating. She said that Elgin complained every winter although it was she not he who bought the fuel and stoked the blaze.

'He doesn't really want to live like this,' she said, meaning the austere grandeur of their marital home. 'He'd be much happier in a 1930s mock Tudor with underfloor hot air.'

'Then why does he do it?'

'It brings him huge originality value.'

'Do you like it?'

'I made it.' She paused. 'The only thing Elgin's ever put into this house is money.'

'You despise him, don't you?'

'No, I don't despise him. I'm disappointed in him.'

Elgin had been a brilliant medical trainee. He had worked hard and learned well. He had been innovative and concerned. During his early hospital years, when Louise had supported him financially and paid all the bills that accumulated round their modest life together, Elgin had been determined to qualify and work in the Third World. He scorned what he called 'the consultancy trail', where able young men of a certain background put in their minimum share of hospital slog and were promoted up the ladder to easier and better things. There was a fast-track in medicine. Very few women were on it, it was the recognised route of the career doctor.

'So what happened?'

'Elgin's mother got cancer.'

In Stamford Hill Sarah felt sick. She had always got up at five o'clock, prayed and lit the candles, gone to work preparing the day's food and ironing Esau's white shirts. She wore a headscarf in those early hours, only placing her long black wig a few moments before her husband came downstairs at seven. They ate breakfast and together got into their ancient car and drove the three miles to the shop. Sarah mopped the floor and dusted the counter while Esau put his white coat over his prayer shawl and shifted the cardboard boxes in the back room. It cannot truly be said that they opened their shop at nine, rather they unlocked the door. Sarah sold toothbrushes and lozenges. Esau made up paper packets of medicine. They had done so for fifty years.

The shop was unchanged. The mahogany counter and glass cabinets had been where they were since before the war, since before Esau and Sarah bought a sixty-year lease to carry them into old age. On one side of them, the cobbler had become a grocery store had become a delicatessen had become a Kosher Kebab House. On the other side, the take-in laundry had become a dry cleaners. It was still run by the children of their friends the Shiffys.

'Your boy,' said Shiffy to Esau. 'He's a doctor, I saw him in the paper. He could bring a nice practice here. You could expand.'

'I'm seventy-two,' said Esau.

'So you're seventy-two? Think of Abraham, think of Isaac, think of Methuselah. Nine hundred and sixty-nine. That's the time to worry about your age.'

'He's married a shiksa.'

'We all make mistakes. Look at Adam.'

Esau didn't tell Shiffy that he never heard from Elgin any more. He never expected to hear from him again. Two weeks later when Sarah was in hospital unable to speak for the pain, Esau dialled Elgin's number on his Bakelite sit-up-and-beg telephone. They had never bothered to get a later model. God's children had no need of progress.

Elgin came at once and spoke to the doctor before he met his father at the bedside. The doctor said there was no hope. Sarah had cancer of the bone and would not live. The doctor said she must have been in pain for years. Slowly crumbling, dust to dust.

'Does my father know?'

'In a way.' The doctor was busy and had to get on. He gave his notes to Elgin and left him at a desk under a lamp with a blown bulb.

Sarah died. Elgin went to the funeral then took his father back to the shop. Esau fumbled with the keys and opened the heavy door. The glass panel still had the gold lettering that had once announced the signs of Esau's success. The upper arc had said ROSENTHAL and the lower, CHEMIST. Time and the weather had beat upon the sign and although it still declared ROSENTHAL, underneath it now read HE MIST.

Elgin, close behind his father, was sick to the stomach at the smell. It was the smell of his childhood, formaldehyde and peppermint. It was the smell of his homework behind the counter. The long nights waiting for his parents to take him home. Sometimes he fell asleep in his grey socks and shorts, his head on a table of logarithms, then Esau would scoop him up and carry him to the car. He remembered his father's tenderness only through the net of dreams and half-wakefulness. Esau was hard on the boy but when he saw him head down on the table, his thin legs loose against the chair, he loved him and whispered in his ear about the lily of the valley and the Promised Land.

All this cut at Elgin as he watched his father slowly hang his black coat on the peg and shrug his arms into his chemist's uniform. He seemed to take comfort from this regular act, didn't look at Elgin but got out his order book and sat muttering over it. After a while Elgin coughed and said he had to go. His father nodded, wouldn't speak.

'Is there anything I can do for you?' asked Elgin not wanting an answer.

'Can you tell me why your mother died?'

Elgin cleared his throat a second time. He was desperate.

'Father, mother was old, she didn't have the strength to get better.'

Esau rocked his head up and down up and down. 'It was God's will. The Lord giveth and the Lord taketh away. How many times have I said that today?' There was another long silence. Elgin coughed.

'I have to be getting on.'

Esau shuffled back round the counter and dug in a large discoloured jar.

He gave his son a brown paper bag full of lozenges.

'You have a cough my boy. Take these.'

Elgin stuffed the bag in his overcoat pocket and left. He walked as hard as he could away from the Jewish quarter and when he reached a main road he hailed a cab. Before he climbed in he dumped the bag in a bus-stop bin. It was the last time he saw his father.

It's true that when Elgin began, he didn't realise that his obsessional study of carcinoma would bring more substantial benefits to himself than to any of his patients. He used computer simulations to mimic the effects of rapidly multiplying rogue cells. He saw gene therapy as the likeliest way out for a body besieged by itself. It was very sexy medicine. Gene therapy is the frontier world where names and fortunes can be made. Elgin was wooed by an American pharmaceutical company who got him off the shop floor and into a lab. He'd never liked hospitals anyway.

'Elgin', said Louise, 'can no longer wrap a Band-Aid round a cut finger but he can tell you everything there is to know about cancer. Everything except what causes it and how to cure it.'

'That's a bit cynical isn't it?' I said.

'Elgin doesn't care about people. He never sees any people. He hasn't been on a terminal care ward for ten years. He sits in a multi-million pound laboratory in Switzerland for half the year and stares at a computer. He wants to make the big discovery. Get the Nobel prize.'

'There's nothing wrong with ambition.'

She laughed. 'There's a lot wrong with Elgin.'

I wondered if I could live up to Louise.

We lay down together and I followed the bow of her lips with my finger. She had a fine straight nose, severe and demanding.

Her mouth contradicted her nose, not because it wasn't serious, but because it was sensual. It was full, lascivious in its depth, with a touch of cruelty. The nose and the mouth working together produced an odd effect of ascetic sexuality. There was discernment as well as desire in the picture. She was a Roman Cardinal, chaste, but for the perfect choirboy.

Louise's tastes had no place in the late twentieth century where sex is about revealing not concealing. She enjoyed the titillation of suggestion. Her pleasure was in slow certain arousal, a game between equals who might not always choose to be equals. She was not a D.H. Lawrence type; no-one could take Louise with animal inevitability.

It was necessary to engage her whole person. Her mind, her heart, her soul and her body could only be present as two sets of twins. She would not be divided from herself. She preferred celibacy to tupping.

Elgin and Louise no longer made love. She took the spunk out of him now and again but she refused to have him inside her. Elgin accepted this was part of their deal and Louise knew he used prostitutes. His proclivities would have made that inevitable even in a more traditional marriage. His present hobby was to fly up to Scotland and be sunk in a bath of porridge while a couple of Celtic geishas rubber-gloved his prick.

'He wouldn't want to be naked in front of strangers,' said Louise. 'I'm the only person, apart from his mother, who's seen him undressed.'

'Why do you stay with him?'

'He used to be a good friend, that's before he started working all the time. I'd have been happy enough to stay with him and live my own life, except that something happened.'

'What?'

'I saw you in the park. It was a long time before we met.'

I wanted to question her. My heart was beating too fast and I felt both enervated and exhausted, the way I do when I drink without eating. Whatever Louise had to say I wouldn't have been able to cope with it. I lay on my back and watched the shadows from the fire. There was an ornamental palm in the room, its leaves reflected to a grotesque outsize. This was no tame domestic space.

In the hours that followed, waking and sleeping with a light fever that bore on me out of passion and distress, it seemed as if the small room was full of ghosts. There were figures at the window gazing out through the muslin curtains, talking to one another in low voices. A man stood warming himself by the low grate. There was no furniture apart from the bed and the bed was levitating. We were surrounded by hands and faces shifting and connecting, now looming into focus vaporous and large, now disappearing like the bubbles children blow.

The figures assumed shapes I recognised; Inge, Catherine, Bathsheba, Jacqueline. Others of whom Louise knew nothing. They came too close, put their fingers in my mouth, in my nostrils, drew back the hoods of my eyes. They accused me of lies and betrayal. I opened my mouth to speak but I had no tongue only a gutted space. I must have cried out then because I was in Louise's arms and she was bending over me, fingers on my forehead, soothing me, whispering to me. 'I will never let you go.'

How to get back into my flat? I telephoned the Zoo the following morning and asked to speak to Jacqueline. They said she hadn't come in to work. I had a mild temperature and only a pair of shorts at my disposal but I thought it best to try and settle matters with her as soon as I could. No way out but through.

Louise lent me her car. When I got to my flat the curtains were still drawn but the chain was off the door. Cautiously I pushed it open. I half expected Jacqueline to fly at me with the mincer. I stood in the hall and called her name. There was no answer. Strictly speaking Jacqueline didn't live with me. She had her own room in a shared house. She kept certain things in my flat and as far as I could see they were gone. No coat behind the door. No hat or gloves shoved in the hall stand. I tried the bedroom.

It was wrecked. Whatever Jacqueline had done the previous night she hadn't had time to sleep. The room looked like a chicken shed. There were feathers everywhere. The pillows had been ripped, the duvet gutted and emptied. She had torn the drawers from their chests and tipped the contents about like any good burglar. I stood too stunned to make much of it, I bent and picked up a T-shirt then dropped it again. I would have to use it as a duster since she'd cut a hole in the middle. I backed out into the sitting room. That was better, no feathers, nothing broken, simply everything was gone. The table, the chairs, the stereo, the vases and pictures, the glasses, bottles, mirrors and lamps. It was blissfully zen. She had left a bunch of flowers in the middle of the floor. Presumably she couldn't fit them into her car. Her car. Her car was locked up like an accessory after the fact. How had she got away with my things?

I went to pee. It seemed like a sensible move providing that the toilet was still there. It was but she had taken the toilet seat. The bathroom looked like it had been the target of a depraved and sadistic plumber. The taps were twisted on their sides, there was a monkey wrench skewed under the hot water pipe where someone had done their best to disconnect me. The walls were covered in heavy felt-tip pen. It was Jacqueline's handwriting. There was a long list of her attributes over the bath. A longer list of my disabilities over the sink. Pasted like an acid-house frieze around the ceiling was Jacqueline's name over and over again. Jacqueline colliding with Jacqueline. An endless cloning of Jacquelines in black ink. I went and peed in the coffee pot. She didn't like coffee. Staring blearily back at the bathroom door I saw it had SHIT daubed across it. The word and the matter. That explained the smell.

The worm in the bud. That's right, most buds do have worms but what about the ones that turn? I thought Jacqueline would have crept away as quietly as she had crept in.

The wise old hands who advocate a sensible route, not too much passion, not too much sex, plenty of greens and an early night, don't recognise this as a possible ending. In their world good manners and good sense prevail. They don't imagine that to choose sensibly is to set a time-bomb under yourself. They don't imagine you are ripe for the cutting, waiting for your chance at life. They don't think of the wreckage an exploding life will cause. It's not in their rule book even though it happens again and again. Settle down, feet under the table. She's a nice girl, he's a nice boy. It's the clichés that cause the trouble.

I lay down on the hard wooden floor of my new zen sitting room and contemplated a spider throwing a web. Blind nature. Homo sapiens. Unlike Robert the Bruce I had no ingenious revelations only a huge sadness. I'm not the kind who can replace love with convenience or passion with pick-ups. I don't want slippers at home and dancing shoes in a little bed-sit round the block. That's how it's done isn't it? Package up your life with supermarket efficiency, don't mix the heart with the liver.

I've never been the slippers; never been the one to sit at home and desperately believe in another late office meeting. I haven't gone to bed by myself at eleven, pretending to be asleep, ears pricked like a guard dog for the car in the drive. I haven't stretched out my hand to check the clock and felt the cold weight of those lost hours ticking in my stomach.

Plenty of times I've been the dancing shoes and how

those women have wanted to play. Friday night, a weekend conference. Yes, in my flat. Off with the business suit, legs apart, pulling me down on them, a pause for champagne and English cheese. And while we're doing that somebody is looking out of the window watching the weather change. Watching the clock, watching the phone, she said she'd ring after her last session. She does ring. She lifts herself off me and dials the number resting the receiver against her breast. She's wet with sex and sweat. 'Hello darling, yes fine, it's raining outside.'

Turn down the lights. This is outside of time. The edge of a black hole where we can go neither forward nor back. Physicists are speculating on what might happen if we could lodge ourselves on the crater sides of such a hole. It seems that due to the peculiarities of the event horizon we could watch history pass and never become history ourselves. We would be trapped eternally observing with no-one to tell. Perhaps that's where God is, then God will understand the conditions of infidelity.

Don't move. We can't move, caught like lobster in a restaurant aquarium. These are the confines of our life together, this room, this bed. This is the voluptuous exile freely chosen. We daren't eat out, who knows whom we may meet? We must buy food in advance with the canniness of a Russian peasant. We must store it unto the day, chilled in the fridge, baked in the oven. Temperatures of hot and cold, fire and ice, the extremes under which we live.

We don't take drugs, we're drugged out on danger, where to meet, when to speak, what happens when we see each other publicly. We think no-one has noticed but there are always faces at the curtain, eyes on the road. There's nothing to whisper about so they whisper about us.

Turn up the music. We're dancing together tightly sealed like a pair of 50s homosexuals. If anyone knocks at the door we won't answer. If I have to answer we'll say she's my accountant. We can't hear anything but the music smooth as a tube lubricating us round the floor. I've been waiting for her all week. All week has been a regime of clocks and calendars. I thought she might telephone on Thursday to say that she couldn't come, that sometimes happens even though we're only together one weekend in five and those stolen after-office hours.

She arches her body like a cat on a stretch. She nuzzles her cunt into my face like a filly at the gate. She smells of the sea. She smells of rockpools when I was a child. She keeps a starfish in there. I crouch down to taste the salt, to run my fingers around the rim. She opens and shuts like a sea anemone. She's refilled each day with fresh tides of longing.

The sun won't stay behind the blind. The room is flooded with light that makes sine waves on the carpet. The carpet that looked so respectable in the showroom has a harem red to it now. I was told it was burgundy.

She lies against the light resting her back on a rod of light. The light breaks colours under her eyelids. She wants the light to penetrate her, breaking open the dull colds of her soul where nothing has warmed her for more summers than she can count. Her husband lies over her like a tarpaulin. He wades into her as though she were a bog. She loves him and he loves her. They're still married aren't they?

On Sunday, when she's gone, I can open the curtains, wind my watch and clear the dishes stacked round the bed. I can make my supper from the left-overs and think about her at home for Sunday dinner, listening to the gentle ticking of the clock and the sound of busy hands running her a bath. Her husband will feel sorry for her, bags under her eyes, worn out. Poor baby, she hardly got any sleep. Tuck her up in her own sheets, that's nice. I can take our soiled ones to the launderette.

Such things lead the heart-sore to the Jacquelines of this world but the Jacquelines of this world lead to such things. Is there no other way? Is happiness always a compromise?

I used to read women's magazines when I visited the dentist. They fascinate me with their arcane world of sex tips and man-traps. I am informed by the thin glossy pages that the way to tell if your husband is having an affair is to check his underpants and cologne. The magazines insist that when a man finds a mistress he will want to cover his prick more regally than of old. He will want to cover his tracks with a new aftershave. No doubt the magazines know best. There's Mr Right furtively locking the bathroom door to try on his brand new six-pack of boxer shorts (size L). His faithful greying Y-fronts lie discarded on the floor. The bathroom mirror is fixed to give him a good view of his face but to get at the important thing he will have to balance on the edge of the bath and hold on to the shower rail. That's better, now all he can see is an ad from a men's magazine, fine lawn cotton pouched round a firm torso. He jumps down, satisfied, and splashes on a bucket load of Hommage Homme. Mrs Right won't notice, she's cooking a curry.

If Mrs Right is having an affair it will be harder to spot, so the magazines say, and they know best. She won't buy new clothes, in fact, she's likely to dress down so that her husband will believe her when she says she's going to an evening class in mediaeval lute music. Unless she has a career, it will be very difficult for her to get away with it regularly except in the afternoons. Is that why so many women are choosing careers? Is that why Kinsey found that so many prefer sex in the afternoon?

I had a girlfriend once who could only achieve orgasm between the hours of two and five o'clock. She worked in the Botanical Gardens in Oxford where she bred rubber plants. It was tricky work trying to satisfy her, when at any moment a fee-paying visitor with the proper ticket of admission might require advice about *Ficus elastica*. Nevertheless, passion propelled me and I visited her in the depths of winter, muffled from head to foot, stamping rushes of snow from my boots like a character from *Anna Karenina*.

I've always been fond of Vronsky but I don't believe in living out literature. Judith was deeply sunk in Conrad. She sat amongst the rubber plants reading *Heart of Darkness*. The most erotic thing I might have said to her was, 'Mistah Kurtz – he dead.' The Soviets, I am told, suffer extremely from having to wear wrappings of fur when outside, only to shed down to their knickers when inside. This was my problem. Judith lived in a perpetual hot-house world of shorts and T-shirts. I had to carry my skimpy garments with me or risk a dash through the cold aided only by a duffle-coat. One quiet afternoon after sex on the wood chippings beneath a trailing vine, we had a tiff and she locked me out of the greenhouse. I ran from window to window banging vainly at the panes. It was snowing and I was wearing only my Mickey Mouse one-piece.

'If you don't let me in I'll die.'

'Die then.'

I decided I was too young to freeze to death. I ran

through the streets back to my lodgings with as much insouciance as I could muster. An old-age pensioner gave me 50p for rag week and I wasn't arrested. We should be thankful for small mercies. I rang Judith to tell her it was all off and would she return my things?

'I've burnt them,' she said.

Perhaps I'm not meant to have any worldly goods. Perhaps they are blocking my spiritual progress and my higher self continually chooses situations where I will be free of material burdens. It's a comforting thought, slightly better than being a sucker . . . Judith's bottom. I treasure it.

Into the heart of my childish vanities, Louise's face, Louise's words, 'I will never let you go.' This is what I have been afraid of, what I've avoided through so many shaky liaisons. I'm addicted to the first six months. It's the midnight calls, the bursts of energy, the beloved as battery for all those fading cells. I told myself after the last whipping with Bathsheba that I wouldn't do any of it again. I did suspect that I might like being whipped, if so, I had at least to learn to wear an extra overcoat. Jacqueline was an overcoat. She muffled my senses. With her I forgot about feeling and wallowed in contentment. Contentment is a feeling you say? Are you sure it's not an absence of feeling? I liken it to that particular numbness one gets after a visit to the dentist. Not in pain nor out of it, slightly drugged. Contentment is the positive side of resignation. It has its appeal but it's no good wearing an overcoat and furry slippers and heavy gloves when what the body really wants is to be naked.

I never used to think about my previous girlfriends until I took up with Jacqueline. I never had the time.

With Jacqueline I settled into a parody of the sporting colonel, the tweedy cove with a line-up of trophies and a dozen reminiscences about each. I have caught myself fancying a glass of sherry and a little mental dalliance with Inge, Catherine, Bathsheba, Judith, Estelle . . . Estelle, I haven't thought about Estelle for years. She had a scrap metal business. No, no, no! I don't want to go backwards in time like a sci-fi thriller. What is it to me that Estelle had a clapped-out Rolls-Royce with a pneumatic back seat? I can still smell the leather.

Louise's face. Under her fierce gaze my past is burned away. The beloved as nitric acid. Am I hoping for a saviour in Louise? An almighty scouring of deed and misdeed, leaving the slab clean and white. In Japan they do a nice virgin substitute with the white of an egg. For twenty-four hours at least, you can have a new hymen. In Europe we have always preferred a half lemon. Not only does it act as a crude pessary, it also makes it very difficult for the most persistent of men to drop anchor in what may seem the most pliant of women. Tightness passes for newness; the man believes his little bride has satisfyingly sealed depths. He can look forward to plunging her inch by inch.

Cheating is easy. There's no swank to infidelity. To borrow against the trust someone has placed in you costs nothing at first. You get away with it, you take a little more and a little more until there is no more to draw on. Oddly, your hands should be full with all that taking but when you open them there's nothing there.

When I say 'I will be true to you' I am drawing a quiet space beyond the reach of other desires. No-one can legislate love; it cannot be given orders or cajoled into service. Love belongs to itself, deaf to pleading and unmoved by violence. Love is not something you can negotiate. Love is the one thing stronger than desire and the only proper reason to resist temptation. There are those who say that temptation can be barricaded beyond the door. The ones who think that stray desires can be driven out of the heart like the moneychangers from the temple. Maybe they can, if you patrol your weak points day and night, don't look don't smell, don't dream. The most reliable Securicor, church sanctioned and state approved, is marriage. Swear you'll cleave only unto him or her and magically that's what will happen. Adultery is as much about disillusionment as it is about sex. The charm didn't work. You paid all that money, ate the cake and it didn't work. It's not *your* fault is it?

Marriage is the flimsiest weapon against desire. You may as well take a pop-gun to a python. A friend of mine, a banker and a very rich man who had travelled the world, told me he was getting married. I was surprised because I knew that for years he had been obsessed with a dancer who for wild and proper reasons of her own wouldn't commit. Finally he had lost patience and chosen a pleasant steady girl who ran a riding school. I saw him at his flat the weekend before his wedding. He told me how serious he was about marriage, how he had read the wedding service and found it beautiful. Within its confines he sensed happiness. Just then the doorbell rang and he took receipt of a van-load of white lilies. He was arranging them enthusiastically and telling me his theories on love, when the doorbell rang again and he took receipt of a crate of Veuve Clicquot and a huge tin of caviare. He had the table set and I noticed how often he looked at his watch.

'After we're married,' he said, 'I can't imagine wanting another woman.' The doorbell rang a third time. It was the dancer. She had come for the weekend. 'I'm not married yet,' he said.

When I say 'I will be true to you' I must mean it in spite of the formalities, instead of the formalities. If I commit adultery in my heart then I have lost you a little. The bright vision of your face will blur. I may not notice this once or twice, I may pride myself on having enjoyed those fleshy excursions in the most cerebral way. Yet I will have blunted that sharp flint that sparks between us, our desire for one another above all else.

King Kong. The huge gorilla is at the top of the Empire State Building holding Fay Wray in the palm of his hand. A bevy of aircraft have been sent to wound the monster but he brushes them away as you would a fly. In the grip of desire a two-seater bi-plane with MARRIED on the side will hardly scratch the beast. You'll still lie awake at night twisting your wedding ring round and round.

With Louise I want to do something different. I want the holiday and the homecoming together. She is the edge and the excitement for me but I have to believe it beyond six months. My circadian clock, which puts me to sleep at night and wakes me up in the morning in a regular twenty-four-hour fashion, has a larger arc that seems set at twenty-four weeks. I can override it, I've managed that, but I can't stop it going off. With Bathsheba, my longest love at three years, the faithful ticker was cheated. She was so little there that while she occupied a fair stretch of time, she filled my days hardly at all. That may have been her secret. If she had lain with me and eaten with me and washed scrubbed and bathed with me, maybe I'd have been off in six months, or at least itching. I think she knew that.

So what affects the circadian clock? What interrupts it, slows it, speeds it? These questions occupy an obscure branch of science called chronobiology. Interest in the clock is growing because as we live more and more artificially, we'd like to con nature into altering her patterns for us. Night-workers and frequent fliers are absolutely the victims of their stubborn circadian clocks. Hormones are deep in the picture, so are social factors and environmental ones. Emerging from this melée, bit by bit, is light. The amount of light to which we are exposed crucially affects our clock. Light. Sun like a disc-saw through the body. Shall I submit myself sundial-wise beneath Louise's direct gaze? It's a risk; human beings go mad without a little shade, but how to break the habit of a lifetime else?

Louise took my face between her hands. I felt her long fingers tapering the sides of my head, her thumbs under my jawbone. She drew me to her, kissing me gently, her tongue inside my lower lip. I put my arms around her, not sure whether I was a lover or a child. I wanted her to hide me beneath her skirts against all menace. Sharp points of desire were still there but there was too a sleepy safe rest like being in a boat I had as a child. She rocked me against her, sea-calm, sea under a clear sky, a glass-bottomed boat and nothing to fear.

'The wind's getting up,' she said.

Louise let me sail in you over these spirited waves. I have the hope of a saint in a coracle. What made them set out in years before the year 1000 with nothing between themselves and the sea but pieces of leather and lath? What made them certain of another place uncharted and unseen? I can see them now, eating black bread and honeycomb, sheltering from the rain under an animal hide. Their bodies are weathered but their souls are transparent. The sea is a means not an end. They trust it in spite of the signs.

The earliest pilgrims shared a cathedral for a heart. They were the temple not made with hands. The Eklasia of God. The song that carried them over the waves was the hymn that rung the rafters. Their throats were bare for God. Look at them now, heads thrown back, mouths open, alone but for the gulls that dip the prow. Against the too salt sea and the inhospitable sky, their voices made a screen of praise.

Love it was that drove them forth. Love that brought them home again. Love hardened their hands against the oar and heated their sinews against the rain. The journeys they made were beyond common sense; who leaves the hearth for the open sea? especially without a compass, especially in winter, especially alone. What you risk reveals what you value. In the presence of love, hearth and quest become one.

Louise, I would gladly fire the past for you, go and not look back. I have been reckless before, never counting the cost, oblivious to the cost. Now, I've done the sums ahead. I know what it will mean to redeem myself from the accumulations of a lifetime. I know and I don't care. You set before me a space uncluttered by association. It might be a void or it might be a release. Certainly I want to take the risk. I want to take the risk because the life I have stored up is going mouldy.

She kissed me and in her kiss lay the complexity of passion. Lover and child, virgin and roué. Had I ever been kissed before? I was as shy as an unbroken colt. I had Mercutio's swagger. This was the woman I had made love with yesterday, her taste was fresh on my mouth, but would she stay? I quivered like a schoolgirl.

'You're shaking,' she said.

'I must be cold.'

'Let me warm you.'

We lay down on my floor, our backs to the day. I needed no more light than was in her touch, her fingers brushing my skin, bringing up the nerve ends. Eyes closed I began a voyage down her spine, the cobbled road of hers that brought me to a cleft and a damp valley then a deep pit to drown in. What other places are there in the world than those discovered on a lover's body?

We were quiet together after we had made love. We watched the afternoon sun fall across the garden, the long shadows of early evening making patterns on the white wall. I was holding Louise's hand, conscious of it, but sensing too that a further intimacy might begin, the recognition of another person that is deeper than consciousness, lodged in the body more than held in the mind. I didn't understand that sensing, I wondered if it might be bogus, I'd never known it myself although I'd seen it in a couple who'd been together for a very long time. Time had not diminished their love. They seemed to have become one another without losing their very individual selves. Only once had I seen it and I envied it. The odd thing about Louise, being with Louise, was déjà vu. I couldn't know her well and yet I did know her well. Not facts and figures, I was endlessly curious about her life, rather a particular trust. That afternoon, it seemed to me I had always been here with Louise, we were familiar.

'I've spoken to Elgin,' she said. 'I told him what you are to me. I told him we'd been to bed together.'

'What did he say?'

'He asked which bed.'

'Which bed?'

'Our marital bed, as I suppose he'd call it, was made by him when we were living on my money in a tiny house. He was training, I was teaching, he made the bed in the evenings . . . It's very uncomfortable. I told him we'd used my bed. The Lady's Occasional . . . He was calmer then.'

I could understand how Elgin felt about his bed. Bathsheba had always insisted that we use their marital bed. I had to sleep on his side. It was the violation of innocence I objected to, a bed should be a safe place. It's not safe if you can't turn your back before it's occupied again. I air my scruples now but it didn't stop me at the time. I do despise myself for that.

'I told Elgin I had to be able to see you, to be free to come and go with you. I told him I wouldn't lie and that I didn't want him to lie to me . . . He asked me if I was going to leave him and I said I honestly didn't know.'

She turned to me her face serious and disturbed. 'I honestly don't know. Do you want me to leave him?'

I swallowed and struggled hard for the answer. The answer in my throat coming straight from my heart was 'Yes. Pack now.' I couldn't say that, I made my answer from my head.

'Shall we see how we go?'

Louise's face betrayed her for a second only but I knew that she too had wanted me to say yes. I tried to help us both.

'We could decide in three months. That would be fairer wouldn't it? To Elgin, to you?'

'What about you?'

I shrugged. 'I've done with Jacqueline. I'm here for you if you want me.'

She said, 'I want to offer you more than infidelity.'

I looked into her lovely face and I thought, I'm not ready for this. My boots are still muddy from the time before. I said, 'Yesterday you were angry with me, you accused me of trophy hunting and you told me not to declare my love to you until I had declared it to myself. You were right. Give me time to do the work I must do. Don't make it easy for me. I want to be sure. I want you to be sure.'

She nodded. 'When I saw you two years ago I thought you were the most beautiful creature male or female I had ever seen.'

Two years ago, what was she talking about?

'I saw you in the park, you were walking by yourself, you were talking to yourself. I followed you for about an hour and then I went home. I never imagined to see you again. You were a game in my head.'

'Do you often follow people in the park?'

She laughed. 'Never before and only once since. The second time I saw you. You were in the British Library.'

'Translating?'

'Yes. I noted your seat number and I asked the desk clerk if he knew your name. When I had your name I found your address and that is why six months ago you found a drenched distressed creature in the road beyond your door.'

'You told me you had had your bag stolen.'

'Yes.'

'You asked me if I could let you dry off and phone your husband.'

'Yes.'

'None of that was real?'

'I had to speak to you. It was the only thing I could think of. Not very clever. And then I met Jacqueline and I thought I must stop and I thought about Elgin and tried to stop. I lured myself into believing that we could be friends, if I was your friend that would be enough. We made good friends, didn't we?'

I dwelt on that day when I had found Louise in the rain. She looked like Puck sprung from the mist. Her hair was shining with bright drops of rain, the rain ran down her breasts, their outline clear through her wet muslin dress.

'It was Emma, Lady Hamilton, who gave me the idea,' said Louise, stealing my thoughts. 'She used to wet her dress before she went out. It was very provocative but it worked on Nelson.'

Not Nelson again.

Yes, that day. I saw her from my bedroom window and rushed out. It was an act of kindness on my part but a very delightful one. It was I who had telephoned her the following day. She very kindly invited me to lunch. All that I could follow, what I couldn't follow was the spring of her motive. I don't lack self-confidence but I'm not beautiful, that is a word reserved for very few people, people such as Louise herself. I told her this.

'You can't see what I can see.' She stroked my face. 'You are a pool of clear water where the light plays.'

There was a hammering at the door. We both jumped.

'It must be Jacqueline,' said Louise. 'I thought she'd be back when it got dark.'

'She's not a vampire.'

The hammering stopped then a key was inserted carefully into the lock. Had Jacqueline been checking to see if anyone was home? I heard her come in and go into the bedroom. Then she opened the sitting room door. She saw Louise and burst into tears.

'Jacqueline, why did you steal my stuff?'

'I hate you.'

I tried to persuade her to sit down and have a drink but as soon as she'd taken the glass she threw it at Louise. It missed and shattered on the wall behind. She leapt across the room and took one of the sharpest largest pieces and made for Louise's face. I grabbed Jacqueline's wrist and twisted it back against her arm. She cried out and dropped the glass.

'Out,' I said, still holding her. 'Give me the keys and get out.' It was as if I'd never cared for her at all. I wanted to wipe her away. I wanted to blot out her blazing stupid face. She didn't deserve this, in a corner of my mind I knew it was my weakness not hers that had brought us to this shameful day. I should have smoothed things down, parried, instead I slapped her across the face and tore my keys from her pocket.

'That was for the bathroom,' I said as she felt her bleeding mouth. Jacqueline stumbled towards the door and spat in my face. I took her by the collar and frog-marched her to her car. She skidded away without her lights on.

I stood watching her go, hands limp at my sides. I groaned and sat on the low wall beside my flat. The air was cool and calming. Why had I hit her? I'd always prided myself on being the superior partner, the intelligent sensitive one who rated good manners and practised them. Now I'd shown myself to be a cheap thug in a scrap.

She'd angered me and I'd responded by thumping her. How many times does that turn up in the courts? How many times have I curled my lip at other people's violence? I put my head in my hands and cried. This ugliness was my doing. Another failed relationship, another hurt human being. When was I going to stop? I pulled my knuckles along the rough brick. There's always an excuse, a good reason for behaving as we do. I couldn't think of a good reason.

'All right,' I said to myself. 'This is your last chance. If you're worth anything show it now. Be worth Louise.'

I went back inside. Louise was sitting very still looking at the glass between her hands as though it were a crystal ball.

'Forgive me,' I said.

'You didn't hit me.' She turned to me, her full lips in a long straight line. 'If you ever do hit me I shall leave you.'

My stomach contracted. I wanted to defend myself but I couldn't start to say anything. I didn't trust my voice.

Louise got up and went to the bathroom. I didn't warn her. I heard her open the door and draw in her breath sudden and sharp. She came back and held out her hand. We spent the rest of the night cleaning.

The interesting thing about a knot is its formal complexity. Even the simplest pedigree knot, the trefoil, with its three roughly symmetrical lobes, has mathematical as well as artistic beauty. For the religious, King Solomon's knot is said to embody the essence of all knowledge. For carpet makers and cloth weavers all over the world, the challenge of the knot lies in the rules of its surprises. Knots can change but they must be well-behaved. An informal knot is a messy knot.

Louise and I were held by a single loop of love.
The cord passing round our bodies had no sharp twists
or sinister turns. Our wrists were not tied and there was
no noose about our necks. In Italy in the fourteenth and
fifteenth centuries a favourite sport was to fasten two
fighters together with a strong rope and let them beat
each other to death. Often it was death because the loser
couldn't back off and the victor rarely spared him. The
victor kept the rope and tied a knot in it. He had only
to swing it through the streets to terrify money from
passers-by.

I don't want to be your sport nor you to be mine. I
don't want to punch you for the pleasure of it, tangling
the clear lines that bind us, forcing you to your knees,
dragging you up again. The public face of a life in chaos.
I want the hoop around our hearts to be a guide not a
terror. I don't want to pull you tighter than you can bear.
I don't want the lines to slacken either, the thread paying
out over the side, enough rope to hang ourselves.

I was sitting in the library writing this to Louise,
looking at a facsimile of an illuminated manuscript, the
first letter a huge L. The L woven into shapes of birds
and angels that slid between the pen lines. The letter was a
maze. On the outside, at the top of the L, stood a pilgrim
in hat and habit. At the heart of the letter, which had been
formed to make a rectangle out of the double of itself, was
the Lamb of God. How would the pilgrim try through the
maze, the maze so simple to angels and birds? I tried to
fathom the path for a long time but I was caught at dead
ends by beaming serpents. I gave up and shut the book,
forgetting that the first word had been Love.

In the weeks that followed Louise and I were together as much as we could be. She was careful with Elgin, I was careful with both of them. The carefulness was wearing us out.

One night, after a seafood lasagne and a bottle of champagne we made love so vigorously that the Lady's Occasional was driven across the floor by the turbine of our lust. We began by the window and ended by the door. It's well-known that molluscs are aphrodisiac, Casanova ate his mussels raw before pleasuring a lady but then he also believed in the stimulating powers of hot chocolate.

Articulacy of fingers, the language of the deaf and dumb, signing on the body body longing. Who taught you to write in blood on my back? Who taught you to use your hands as branding irons? You have scored your name into my shoulders, referenced me with your mark. The pads of your fingers have become printing blocks, you tap a message on to my skin, tap meaning into my body. Your morse code interferes with my heart beat. I had a steady heart before I met you, I relied upon it, it had seen active service and grown strong. Now you alter its pace with your own rhythm, you play upon me, drumming me taut.

Written on the body is a secret code only visible in certain lights; the accumulations of a lifetime gather there. In places the palimpsest is so heavily worked that the letters feel like braille. I like to keep my body rolled up away from prying eyes. Never unfold too much, tell the whole story. I didn't know that Louise would have reading hands. She has translated me into her own book.

We tried to be quiet for Elgin's sake. He had arranged to be out but Louise thought he was at home. In silence and in darkness we loved each other and as I traced her bones with my palm I wondered what time would do to skin that was so new to me. Could I ever feel any less for this body? Why does ardour pass? Time that withers you will wither me. We will fall like ripe fruit and roll down the grass together. Dear friend, let me lie beside you watching the clouds until the earth covers us and we are gone.

Elgin was at breakfast the following morning. This was a shock. He was as pale as his shirt. Louise slid into her place at the foot of the long table. I took up a neutral position about half way. I buttered a slice of toast and bit. The noise vibrated the table. Elgin winced.

'Do you have to make so much noise?'

'Sorry Elgin,' I said, spattering the cloth with crumbs.

Louise passed me the teapot and smiled.

'What are you so happy about?' said Elgin. 'You didn't get any sleep either.'

'You told me you were away until today,' said Louise quietly.

'I came home. It's my house. I paid for it.'

'It's our house and I told you we'd be here last night.'

'I might as well have slept in a brothel.'

'I thought that's what you were doing,' said Louise.

Elgin got up and threw his napkin on the table. 'I'm exhausted but I'm going to work. Lives depend on my work and because of you I shall not be at my best today. You might think of yourself as a murderer.'

'I might but I shan't,' said Louise.

We heard Elgin clatter his mountain bike out of the hall. Through the basement window I saw him strap on his pink helmet. He liked cycling, he thought it was good for his heart.

Louise was lost in thought. I drank two cups of tea, washed up and was thinking of going home when she put her arms around me from behind and rested her chin on my shoulder.

'This isn't working,' she said.

She asked me to wait three days and promised to send me a message after that time. I nodded, dog-dumb, and went back to my corner. I was hopelessly in love with Louise and very scared. I spent the three days trying again to rationalise us, to make a harbour in the raging sea where I could bob about and admire the view. There was no view, only Louise's face. I thought of her as intense and beyond common sense. I never knew what she would do next. I was still loading on to her all my terror. I still wanted her to be the leader of our expedition. Why did I find it hard to accept that we were equally sunk? Sunk in each other? Destiny is a worrying concept. I don't want to be fated, I want to choose. But perhaps Louise had to be chosen. If the choice is as crude as Louise or not Louise then there is no choice.

I sat in the library on the first day trying to work on my translations but jotting on the blotter the line of my true enquiry. I was sick to the gut with fear. The heavy fear of not seeing her again. I wouldn't break my word. I wouldn't go to the phone. I scanned the row of industrious heads. Dark, blonde, grey, bald, wig. A long way round was a bright red flame. I knew it wasn't Louise but I couldn't take my eyes off the colour. It soothed me the way any bear will soothe a child not at home. It wasn't mine but it was like mine. If I made my eyes into narrow slits the red took up the whole room. The dome was lit with red. I felt like a seed in a pomegranate. Some say that the pomegranate was the real apple of Eve, fruit of the womb, I would eat my way into perdition to taste you.

'I love her what can I do?'

The gentleman in the knitted waistcoat opposite looked up and frowned. I had broken the rule and spoken out loud. Worse, I had spoken to myself. I gathered my books and rushed from the room, past the suspicious gaze of the guards and out down the steps built through the massive columns of the British Museum. I started to walk home, convincing myself that I would never hear from Louise again. She would go to Switzerland with Elgin and have a baby. A year ago Louise had given up her job at Elgin's request so that they could start a family. She had miscarried once and had no wish to do it again. She told me she was firm about no baby. Did I believe her? She had given the one reason I believe. She said, 'It might look like Elgin.'

Reason. I was caught in a Piranesi nightmare. The logical paths the proper steps led nowhere. My mind took me up tortuous staircases that opened into doors that opened into nothing. I knew my problem was partly old war wounds playing up. Put in a situation that smelt anything like the one with Bathsheba and I hit out. Bathsheba had always been asking for time to make definite decisions only to come back with a list of compromises. Louise, I knew, wouldn't make compromises. She would vanish.

Ten years of marriage is a lot of marriage. I can't be relied upon to describe Elgin properly. More importantly I'd never met the other Elgin, the one she'd married. No-one whom Louise had loved could be worthless, if I believed that I'd have to accept that I might be worthless too. At least I had never pressured her to leave. It would be her own decision.

I had a boyfriend once called Crazy Frank. He had been brought up by midgets although he himself was over six feet tall. He loved his adopted parents and used to carry them one on each shoulder. I met him doing exactly that at a Toulouse-Lautrec exhibition in Paris. We went to a bar and then on to another bar and got very drunk and while we were in a shot bed in a cheap pension he told me about his passion for miniatures.

'You'd be perfect if you were smaller,' he said.

I asked him if he took his parents everywhere with him and he said that he did. They didn't need much room and they helped him to make friends. He explained that he was very shy.

Frank had the body of a bull, an image he intensified by wearing great gold hoops through his nipples. Unfortunately he had joined the hoops with a chain of heavy gold links. The effect should have been deeply butch but in fact it looked rather like the handle of a Chanel shopping bag.

He didn't want to settle down. His ambition was to find a hole in every port. He wasn't fussy about the precise location. Frank believed that love had been invented to fool people. His theory was sex and friendship. 'Don't people always behave better towards their friends than their lovers?' He warned me never to fall in love, although his words came too late because I had already fallen for him. He was the perfect vagabond, swag bag in one hand, waving with the other. He never stayed anywhere long, he was only in Paris for two months. I begged him to come back to England with me but he laughed and said England was for married couples. 'I have to be free,' he said.

'But you take your parents wherever you go.'

Frank left for Italy and I came home to England. I was torn with grief for two whole days and then

I thought, A man and his midgets. Was that what I wanted? A man whose chest jewellery rattled when he walked?

It was years ago but I still blush. Sex can feel like love or maybe it's guilt that makes me call sex love. I've been through so much I should know just what it is I'm doing with Louise. I should be a grown-up by now. Why do I feel like a convent virgin?

The second day of my ordeal I took a pair of handcuffs to the library with me and locked myself to my seat. I gave the key to the gentleman in the knitted waistcoat and asked him to let me free at five o'clock. I told him I had a deadline, that if I didn't finish my translation a Soviet writer might fail to find asylum in Great Britain. He took the key and said nothing but I noticed he'd disappeared from his place after about an hour.

I worked on, the concentrated silence of the library giving me some release from thoughts of Louise. Why is the mind incapable of deciding its own subject matter? Why when we desperately want to think of one thing do we invariably think of another? The overriding arch of Louise had distracted me from all other constructs. I like mental games, I find it easy to work and I work quickly. In the past whatever my situation I have been able to find peace in work. Now that facility had deserted me. I was a street yob who had to be kept locked up.

Whenever the word Louise came into my mind I replaced it with a brick wall. After a few hours of this my mind was nothing but brick walls. Worse, my left hand was swelling up, I don't think it was getting enough blood being strapped to the chair leg. There was no sign of the gentleman. I signalled to a guard and whispered my problem. He returned with a fellow guard and together they picked up my chair and carried me sedan style down the British Library Reading Room. It is a tribute to the scholarly temperament that nobody looked up.

In the supervisor's office I tried to explain.

'You a Communist?' he said.

'No I'm a floating voter.'

He had me cut loose and charged me for Wilful Damage To Reading Room Chair. I tried to make him amend that to 'accidental damage' but he wouldn't. Then he filed his report very solemnly and told me I'd have to hand over my ticket.

'I can't hand over my ticket. It's my livelihood.'

'Should a thought a that before you handcuffed yourself to Library Property.'

I gave him my ticket and got an appeal form. Could I fall any lower?

The answer was yes. I spent the whole night prowling outside Louise's house like a private dick. I watched the lights going off at some windows, on at others. Was she in his bed? What did that have to do with me? I ran a schizophrenic dialogue with myself through the hours of darkness and into the small hours, so called because the heart shrivels up to the size of a pea and there is no hope left in it.

By morning I was home shivering and wretched. I welcomed the shivering since I hoped it might portend a fever. If I were delirious for a few days her leaving me might hurt less. With luck I might even die. 'Men have died from time to time and worms have eaten them, but not for love.' Shakespeare was wrong, I was living proof of that.

'You ought to be dead proof,' I said to myself. 'If you're living proof he was right.'

I sat down to make a will leaving everything to Louise. Was I in sound mind and body? I took my temperature. No. I peered at my head in the mirror. No. Better go to bed close the curtains and get out the gin bottle.

That was how Louise found me at 6 o'clock on the evening of the third day. She'd been telephoning since noon but I had been too sodden to notice.

'They've taken my ticket away,' I said when I saw her.

I burst into tears and lay blubbering in her arms. There was nothing she could do except give me a bath and a sleeping draught. In my sinking haze I heard her say, 'I will never let you go.'

No-one knows what forces draw two people together. There are plenty of theories; astrology, chemistry, mutual need, biological drive. Magazines and manuals worldwide will tell you how to pick the perfect partner. Dating agencies stress the science of their approach although having a computer does not make one a scientist. The old music of romance is played out in modern digital ways. Why leave yourself to chance when you could leave yourself to science? Shortly the pseudo-lab coat approach of dating by details will make way for a genuine experiment whose results, however unusual, will remain controllable. Or so they say. (See splitting the atom, gene therapy, in vitro fertilisation, cross hormone cultures, even the humble cathode ray for similar statements.) Never mind. Virtual Reality is on its way.

At present to enter a virtual world you would have to put on a crude-looking diving helmet of the kind people used to wear in the 1940s and a special glove rather like a heavy gardening gauntlet. Thus equipped you would be inside a 360° television set with a three-dimensional programme, three-dimensional sound, and solid objects that you could pick up and move around. No longer would you be watching a film from a fixed perspective, this is a film-set you can explore, even alter if you don't like it. As far as your senses can tell you are in a real world. The fact that you are in a diving helmet wearing a gardening glove won't matter.

In a little while, the equipment will be replaced by a room that you can walk into like any other. Except that it will be an intelligent space. The room will be a wall-to-wall virtual world of your choosing. If you like, you may live in a computer-created world all day and all night. You will be able to try out a Virtual life with a Virtual lover. You can go into your Virtual house and do Virtual housework, add a baby or two, even find out if you'd rather be gay. Or single. Or straight. Why hesitate when you could simulate?

And sex? Certainly. Teledildonics is the word. You will be able to plug in your telepresence to the billion-bundle network of fibre optics criss-crossing the world and join your partner in Virtuality. Your real selves will be wearing body suits made up of thousands of tiny tactile detectors per square inch. Courtesy of the fibreoptic network these will receive and transmit touch. The Virtual epidermis will be as sensitive as your own outer layer of skin.

For myself, unreconstructed as I am, I'd rather hold you in my arms and walk through the damp of a real English meadow in real English rain. I'd rather travel across the world to have you with me than lie at home dialling your telepresence. The scientists say I can choose but how much choice have I over their other inventions? My life is not my own, shortly I shall have to haggle over my reality. Luddite? No, I don't want to smash the machines but neither do I want the machines to smash me.

August. The street like a hotplate cooking us. Louise had brought me to Oxford to get away from Elgin. She didn't tell me what had happened in the previous three days, she kept her secret like a war-time agent. She was smiling, calm, the perfect undercover girl. I didn't trust her. I believed she was about to break it off with me, that she had made it up with Elgin and begged this Roman holiday as a way out with a frisson of regret. My chest was full of stones.

We walked, swam in the river, read back to back as lovers do. Talked all the time about everything except ourselves. We were in a Virtual world where the only taboo was real life. But in a true Virtual world I could have gently picked up Elgin and dropped him for ever from the frame. I saw him from the corner of my eye waiting waiting. Elgin squatted over life until it moved.

We were in our rented room, the windows wide open against the heat. Outside, the dense noises of summer; shouts from the street, a click of a croquet ball, laughter, sudden and incomplete and above us Mozart on a tinkly piano. A dog, woof woof woof, chasing the lawn mower. I had my head on your belly and I could hear your lunch on its way to your bowels.

You said, 'I'm going to leave.'

I thought, Yes, of course you are, you're going back to the shell.

You said, 'I'm going to leave him because my love for you makes any other life a lie.'

I've hidden those words in the lining of my coat. I take them out like a jewel thief when no-one's watching. They haven't faded. Nothing about you has faded. You are still the colour of my blood. You are my blood. When I look in the mirror it's not my own face I see. Your body is twice. Once you once me. Can I be sure which is which?

We went home to my flat and you brought nothing from your other life but the clothes you stood up in. Elgin had insisted that you take nothing until the divorce settlement had been agreed. You had asked him to divorce you for Adultery and he had insisted it was to be Unreasonable Behaviour.

'It will help him to save face,' you said. 'Adultery is for cuckolds. Unreasonable Behaviour is for martyrs. A mad wife is better than a bad wife. What will he tell his friends?'

I don't know what he told his friends but I know what he told me. Louise and I had been living together in great happiness for nearly five months. It was Christmas time and we had decorated the flat with garlands of holly and ivy woven from the woods. We had very little money; I had not been translating as much as I should have been and Louise could not resume work until the new year. She'd found a job teaching Art History. Nothing mattered to us. We were insultingly happy. We sang and played and walked for miles looking at buildings and watching people. A treasure had fallen into our hands and the treasure was each other.

Those days have a crystalline clearness to me now. Whichever way I hold them up to the light they refract a different colour. Louise in her blue dress gathering fir cones in the skirt. Louise against the purple sky looking like a Pre-Raphaelite heroine. The young green of our life and the last yellow roses in November. The colours blur and I can only see her face. Then I hear her voice crisp and white. 'I will never let you go.'

It was Christmas Eve and Louise went to visit her mother who had always hated Elgin until Louise told her she was divorcing him. Louise hoped that the season of goodwill might work in her favour and so when the stars were hard and bright she wrapped her mane around her and set off. I waved, smiling, how fine she would look on the Steppes of Russia.

As I was about to close the door, a shadow came towards me. It was Elgin. I didn't want to invite him in but he was menacing in an unlikely jovial way. My neck prickled like an animal's. I thought for Louise's sake I must get it over with.

I gave him a drink and he talked aimlessly until I could bear it no longer. I asked him what he wanted. Was it about the divorce? 'In a way,' he said smiling. 'I think there's something you should know. Something Louise won't have told you.'

'Louise tells me everything,' I said coldly. 'As I do her.'

'Very touching,' he said watching the ice in his Scotch. 'Then you won't be surprised to hear she's got cancer?'

Two hundred miles from the surface of the earth there is no gravity. The laws of motion are suspended. You could turn somersaults slowly slowly, weight into weightlessness, nowhere to fall. As you lay on your back paddling in space you might notice your feet had fled your head. You are stretching slowly slowly, getting longer, your joints are slipping away from their usual places. There is no connection between your shoulder and your arm. You will break up bone by bone, fractured from who you are, you are drifting away now, the centre cannot hold.

Where am I? There is nothing here I recognise. This isn't the world I know, the little ship I've trimmed and rigged. What is this slow-motion space, my arm moving up and down up and down like a parody of Mussolini? Who is this man with the revolving eyes, his mouth opening like a gas chamber, his words acrid, vile, in my throat and nostrils? The room stinks. The air is bad. He's poisoning me and I can't get away. My feet don't obey me. Where is the familiar ballast of my life? I am fighting helplessly without hope. I grapple but my body slithers away. I want to brace myself against something solid but there's nothing solid here.

The facts Elgin. The facts.
  Leukaemia.
  Since when?
  About two years.
  She's not ill.
  Not yet.
  What kind of leukaemia?
  Chronic lymphocytic leukaemia.
  She looks well.
  The patient may have no symptoms for some time.
  She's well.
  I took a blood count after her first miscarriage.
  Her first?
  She was badly anaemic.
  I don't understand.
  It's rare.
  She's not ill.
  Her lymph nodes are now enlarged.

Will she die?
They're rubbery but painless.
Will she die?
Her spleen isn't enlarged at all. That's good.
Will she die?
She has too many white T-cells.
Will she die?
That depends.
On what?
On you.
You mean I can look after her?
I mean I can.

Elgin left and I sat under the Christmas tree watching the swinging angels and the barleysugar candles. His plan was simple: if Louise came back to him he would give her the care money can't buy. She would go with him to Switzerland and have access to the very latest medico-technology. As a patient, no matter how rich, she would not be able to do that. As Elgin's wife she would.

Cancer treatment is brutal and toxic. Louise would normally be treated with steroids, massive doses to induce remission. When her spleen started to enlarge she might have splenic irridation or even a splenectomy. By then she would be badly anaemic, suffering from deep bruising and bleeding, tired and in pain most of the time. She would be constipated. She would be vomiting and nauseous. Eventually chemotherapy would contribute to failure of her bone marrow. She would be very thin, my beautiful girl, thin and weary and lost. There is no cure for chronic lymphocytic leukaemia.

Louise came home her face shining with frost. There was a

deep glow in her cheeks, her lips were icy when she kissed
me. She pushed her frozen hands under my shirt and held
them against my back like two branding irons. She was
chattering about the cold and the stars and how clear the
sky was and the moon hung in an icicle from the roof of
the world.

I didn't want to cry, I wanted to talk to her calmly
and gently. But I did cry, fast hot tears falling on to her
cold skin, scalding her with my misery. Unhappiness is
selfish, grief is selfish. For whom are the tears? Perhaps
it can be no other way.

'Elgin's been here,' I said. 'He told me you have cancer
of the blood.'

'It's not serious.' She said this quickly. What did she
expect me to do?

'Cancer's not serious?'

'I'm asymptomatic.'

'Why didn't you tell me? Couldn't you have told me?'

'It's not serious.'

There is a silence between us for the first time. I
want to be angry with her now. I was pent-up with
rage.

'I was waiting for the results. I've had some more
tests done. I haven't got the results yet.'

'Elgin has, he says you don't want to know.'

'I don't trust Elgin. I'm having a second opinion.'

I was staring at her, my fists clenched so that I could
dig my nails into my palms. When I looked at her I saw
Elgin's square spectacled face. Not Louise's curved lips
but his triumphant mouth.

'Shall I tell you about it?' she said.

In the hours of the night until the sky turned blue-black,

then pearl grey, until the weak winter sun broke on us, we lay in one another's arms wrapped in a travel rug and she told me what she feared and I told her my fears. She would not go back to Elgin, of that she was adamant. She knew a great deal about the disease and I would learn. We would face it together. Brave words and comfort to us both who needed comfort in the small cold room that compassed our life that night. We were setting out with nothing and Louise was ill. She was confident that any costs could be met from her settlement. I was not so sure but too tired and too relieved to go further that night. To reach one another again had been far enough.

The following day when Louise had gone out I went to see Elgin. He seemed to be expecting me. We went into his study. He had a new game on his computer screen. This one was called LABORATORY. A good scientist (played by the operator) and a mad scientist (played by the computer) fight it out to create the world's first transgenic tomato. Implanted with human genes the tomato will make itself into a sandwich, sauce or pizza topping with up to three additional ingredients. But is it ethical?

'Like a game?' he said.

'I've come about Louise.'

He had her test results spread out on a table. The prognosis was about 100 months. He pointed out to me that whilst it was easy for Louise to be careless about her condition as long as she felt fit and well, that would change when she began to lose her strength.

'But why treat her as an invalid before she is an invalid?'

'If we treat her now there is a chance that the disease might be halted. Who knows?' He shrugged and smiled and jangled a few keys on his terminal. The tomato leered.

'Don't you know?'

'Cancer is an unpredictable condition. It is the body turning upon itself. We don't understand that yet. We know what happens but not why it happens or how to stop it.'

'Then you have nothing to offer Louise.'

'Except her life.'

'She won't come back to you.'

'Aren't you both a bit old for the romantic dream?'

'I love Louise.'

'Then save her.'

Elgin sat down at his screen. He considered our interview to be over. 'The trouble is', he said, 'that if I choose the wrong gene I shall get squirted with tomato sauce. You do see my problem.'

Dear Louise,

I love you more than life itself. I have not known a happier time than with you. I did not know this much happiness was possible. Can love have texture? It is palpable to me, the feeling between us, I weigh it in my hands the way I weigh your head in my hands. I hold on to love as a climber does a rope. I knew our path would be steep but I did not foresee the sheer rock face we have come to. We could ascend it, I know that, but it would be you who took the strain.

I'm going away tonight, I don't know where, all I know is I won't come back. You don't have to leave the flat; I have made arrangements there. You are safe in my home but not in my arms. If I stay it will be you who goes, in pain, without help. Our love was not meant to cost you your life. I can't bear that. If it could be my life I would gladly give it. You came to me in the clothes you stood up in, that was enough. No more Louise. No more giving. You have given me everything already.

Please go with Elgin. He has promised to tell me how you are. I shall think of you every day, many times a day. Your hand prints are all over my body. Your flesh is my flesh. You deciphered me and now I am plain to read. The message is a simple one; my love for you. I want you to live. Forgive my mistakes. Forgive me.

I packed and took a train to Yorkshire. I covered my tracks so that Louise could not find me. I took my work and some money that I had, the money left over from paying the mortgage for a year, money enough for a couple of months. I found a tiny cottage and a P.O. Box for my publishers and a friend who had committed to help me. I took a job in a fancy wine bar. A supper bar designed for the nouveau refugees who thought that fish and chips were too working class. We served pommes frites with Dover sole that had never seen a cliff. We served prawns so deeply packed in ice that we sometimes dropped them in a drink by mistake. 'It's a new fashion Sir, Scotch on the rocks à la prawn.' After that everybody wanted one.

My job was to unload coolers of Frascati on to fashionably tiny tables and take the supper order. We offered Mediterranean Special (fish and chips), Pavarotti Special (pizza and chips), Olde Englysshe Special (sausage and chips) and Lovers Special (spare ribs for two with chips and aromatic vinegar). There was an à la carte menu but nobody could find it. All night the handsomely studded green baize door to the kitchens swung back and forth offering a brief glimpse of two busy chefs in hats like steeples.

'Chuck us another pizza Kev.'

'She wants sweetcorn extra.'

'Well give us the tin opener then.'

The ceaseless pinging from the banks of microwaves stacked like a NASA terminal was largely drowned out by the hypnotic thud of the bass speakers in the bar. No-one ever asked how their food was cooked and, had they, they would have been reassured by a postcard of the kitchens signed compliments of the chef. They were not our kitchens but they might have been. The bread was so white it shone.

I bought a bicycle to cover the twenty miles that separated the bar from my rented hovel. I wanted to be too exhausted to think. Still every turn of the wheel was Louise.

My cottage had a table, two chairs, a peg-rug and a bed with a winded mattress. If I needed heat I chopped wood and lit a fire. The cottage had been long abandoned. No-one wanted to live in it and no-one else would have been stupid enough to rent it. There was no telephone and the bath sat in the middle of a semi-partitioned room. The draught wheezed in through a badly boarded up window. The floor creaked like a Hammer horror set. It was dirty, depressing and ideal. The people who owned it thought I was a fool. I am a fool.

There was a greasy armchair by the fire, armchair shrunken inside its loose covers like an old man in a heyday suit. Let me sit in it and never have to get up. I want to rot here, slowly sinking into the faded pattern, invisible against the dead roses. If you could see through the filthy windows you'd see just the back of my head bulging over the line of the chair. You'd see my hair, sparse and thinning, greying, gone. Death's head in the chair, the rose chair in the stagnant garden. What is the point of movement when movement indicates life and life indicates hope? I have neither life nor hope. Better then to fall in with the crumbling wainscot, to settle with the dust and be drawn up into someone's nostrils. Daily we breathe the dead.

What are the characteristics of living things? At school, in biology I was told the following: Excretion, growth, irritability, locomotion, nutrition, reproduction and respiration. This does not seem like a very lively list to me. If that's all there is to being a living thing I may as well be dead. What of that other characteristic prevalent in human living things, the longing to be loved? No, it doesn't come under the heading Reproduction. I have no desire to reproduce but I still seek out love. Reproduction. Over-polished Queen Anne style dining-room suite reduced to clear. Genuine wood. Is that what I want? The model family, two plus two in an easy home assembly kit. I don't want a model, I want the full-scale original. I don't want to reproduce, I want to make something entirely new. Fighting words but the fight's gone out of me.

I tried to clean up a little. I cut some winter jasmine from the ragged garden and brought it indoors. It looked like a nun in a slum. I bought a hammer and some hardboard and patched up the worst of the neglect. I made it so that I could sit over the fire and not feel the wind at the same time. This was an achievement. Mark Twain built a house for himself with a window over the fireplace so that he could watch the snow falling over the flames. I had a hole that let the rain in, but then I had a life that let the rain in.

A few days after I arrived I heard an uncertain yowling outside. A sound that should have been defiant and swagger-all but that wasn't quite. I put on my boots, took a flashlight and stumbled through the January slutch. The mud was deep and viscous. To keep a path to my house I had to strew it daily with ashes. The ashes were choked with mud, the gutter ran straight off the house down to my doorstep. Any gust brought the tiles off the roof.

Flat up against the wall of the house, if sweating pot-bellied brickwork held together with lichen can be called a wall, was a thin mangy cat. It looked at me with eyes composed of hope and fear. It was soaked and shivering. I didn't hesitate, leant down and took it by the scruff of the neck the way Louise had taken me.

Under the light I saw the cat and I were filthy. When had I last taken a bath? My clothes were stale, my skin was grey. My hair fell in defeated flashes. The cat had oil down one flank and mud punking up the fur of its belly.

'It's bathnight in Yorkshire,' I said and took the cat to the tired old enamel tub on three claw feet. The fourth end rested on a copy of the Bible. 'Rock of ages cleft for me. Let me hide myself in thee.' I bullied the ancient boiler into life with a series of screams, pleas, matches and lighter fuel. It finally rumbled and spat, billowing evil-smelling clouds of steam into the peeling bathroom. I could see the cat's eyes, aghast, watching me.

We did get clean, the pair of us, him wrapped in a handtowel, me in my only luxury, a fleecy bathsheet. His head was tiny with the fur plastered against the skull. He had a notch out of one ear and a bad scar over one eye. He trembled in my arms though I spoke to him softly about a bowl of milk. Later, in the collapsing bed, burrowed under an eiderdown so misused that the feathers didn't move when I shook it, a milk-full cat learned to purr. He slept on my chest all night. I didn't sleep much. I tried to keep awake at night until utterly exhausted so that I could miss the early dreaming sleep of one who has much to hide. There are people who starve themselves by day only to find that in the night their denied bodies have savaged the fridge, taken carcasses raw, eaten cat food, toilet paper, anything to satisfy the need.

Sleeping beside Louise had been a pleasure that often led to sex but which was separate from it. The delicious temperate warmth of her body, skin temperature perfect with mine. Moving away from her only to turn over again hours later and mould myself into the curve of her back. Her smell. Specific Louise smell. Her hair. A red blanket to cover us both. Her legs. She never shaved them enough to keep them absolutely smooth. There was a residual roughness that I liked, the very beginning of the hairs growing back. They were not allowed to appear so I didn't discover their colour but I felt them with my feet, pushing my foot down her shin-bone, the long bones of her legs rich in marrow. Marrow where the blood cells are formed red and white. Red and white, the colours of Louise.

In bereavement books they tell you to sleep with a pillow pulled down beside you. Not quite a Dutch wife, that is a bolster held between the legs in the tropics to soak up the sweat, not quite a Dutch wife. 'The pillow will comfort you in the long unbroken hours. If you sleep you will unconsciously benefit from its presence. If you wake the bed will seem less large and lonely.' Who writes these books? Do they really think, those quiet concerned counsellors, that two feet of linen-bound stuffing will assuage a broken heart? I don't want a pillow I want your moving breathing flesh. I want you to hold my hand in the dark, I want to roll on to you and push myself into you. When

I turn in the night the bed is continent-broad. There is endless white space where you won't be. I travel it inch by inch but you're not there. It's not a game, you're not going to leap out and surprise me. The bed is empty. I'm in it but the bed is empty.

I named the cat Hopeful because on the first day he brought me a rabbit and we ate it with lentils. I was able to do some translating work that day and when I got back from the wine bar Hopeful was waiting by the door with an ear cocked and such a look of anticipation that for a moment, a single clear moment, I forgot what I had done. The next day I cycled to the library but instead of going to the Russian section as I had intended I went to the medical books. I became obsessed with anatomy. If I could not put Louise out of my mind I would drown myself in her. Within the clinical language, through the dispassionate view of the sucking, sweating, greedy, defecating self, I found a love-poem to Louise. I would go on knowing her, more intimately than the skin, hair and voice that I craved. I would have her plasma, her spleen, her synovial fluid. I would recognise her even when her body had long since fallen away.

The Cells, Tissues,
Systems and Cavities
of the Body

THE MULTIPLICATION OF CELLS BY MITOSIS OCCURS THROUGH-
OUT THE LIFE OF THE INDIVIDUAL. IT OCCURS AT A MORE RAPID
RATE UNTIL GROWTH IS COMPLETE. THEREAFTER NEW CELLS
ARE FORMED TO REPLACE THOSE WHICH HAVE DIED. NERVE
CELLS ARE A NOTABLE EXCEPTION. WHEN THEY DIE THEY ARE
NOT REPLACED.

In the secret places of her thymus gland Louise is making too much of herself. Her faithful biology depends
on regulation but the white T-cells have turned bandit.
They don't obey the rules. They are swarming into the
bloodstream, overturning the quiet order of spleen and
intestine. In the lymph nodes they are swelling with
pride. It used to be their job to keep her body safe
from enemies on the outside. They were her immunity,
her certainty against infection. Now they are the enemies
on the inside. The security forces have rebelled. Louise is
the victim of a coup.

Will you let me crawl inside you, stand guard over
you, trap them as they come at you? Why can't I dam
their blind tide that filthies your blood? Why are there
no lock gates on the portal vein? The inside of your
body is innocent, nothing has taught it fear. Your artery
canals trust their cargo, they don't check the shipments
in the blood. You are full to overflowing but the keeper
is asleep and there's murder going on inside. Who comes
here? Let me hold up my lantern. It's only the blood; red
cells carrying oxygen to the heart, thrombocytes making

sure of proper clotting. The white cells, B and T types, just a few of them as always whistling as they go.

The faithful body has made a mistake. This is no time to stamp the passports and look at the sky. Coming up behind are hundreds of them. Hundreds too many, armed to the teeth for a job that doesn't need doing. Not needed? With all that weaponry?

Here they come, hurtling through the bloodstream trying to pick a fight. There's no-one to fight but you Louise. You're the foreign body now.

TISSUES, SUCH AS THE LINING OF THE MOUTH, CAN BE SEEN WITH THE NAKED EYE, BUT THE MILLIONS OF CELLS WHICH MAKE UP THE TISSUES ARE SO SMALL THAT THEY CAN ONLY BE SEEN WITH THE AID OF A MICROSCOPE.

The naked eye. How many times have I enjoyed you with my lascivious naked eye. I have seen you unclothed, bent to wash, the curve of your back, the concurve of your belly. I have had you beneath me for examination, seen the scars between your thighs where you fell on barbed wire. You look as if an animal has clawed you, run its steel nails through your skin, leaving harsh marks of ownership.

My eyes are brown, they have fluttered across your body like butterflies. I have flown the distance of your body from side to side of your ivory coast. I know the forests where I can rest and feed. I have mapped you with my naked eye and stored you out of sight. The millions of cells that make up your tissues are plotted on my retina. Night flying I know exactly where I am. Your body is my landing strip.

The lining of your mouth I know through tongue and spit. Its ridges, valleys, the corrugated roof, the fortress of teeth. The glossy smoothness of the inside of your upper lip is interrupted by a rough swirl where you were hurt once. The tissues of the mouth and anus heal faster than any others but they leave signs for those who care to look. I care to look. There's a story trapped inside your mouth. A crashed car and a smashed windscreen. The only witness is the scar, jagged like a duelling scar where the skin still shows the stitches.

My naked eye counts your teeth including the fillings. The incisors, canines, the molars and premolars. Thirty-two in all. Thirty-one in your case. After sex you tiger-tear your food, let your mouth run over with grease. Sometimes it's me you bite, leaving shallow wounds in my shoulders. Do you want to stripe me to match your own? I wear the wounds as a badge of honour. The moulds of your teeth are easy to see under my shirt but the L that tattoos me on the inside is not visible to the naked eye.

FOR DESCRIPTIVE PURPOSES THE HUMAN BODY IS SEPARATED
INTO CAVITIES. THE CRANIAL CAVITY CONTAINS THE BRAIN.
ITS BOUNDARIES ARE FORMED BY THE BONES OF THE SKULL.

Let me penetrate you. I am the archaeologist of tombs. I
would devote my life to marking your passageways, the
entrances and exits of that impressive mausoleum, your
body. How tight and secret are the funnels and wells of
youth and health. A wriggling finger can hardly detect
the start of an ante-chamber, much less push through to
the wide aqueous halls that hide womb, gut and brain.

In the old or ill, the nostrils flare, the eye sockets make
deep pools of request. The mouth slackens, the teeth fall
from their first line of defence. Even the ears enlarge like
trumpets. The body is making way for worms.

As I embalm you in my memory, the first thing I shall
do is to hook out your brain through your accommodat-
ing orifices. Now that I have lost you I cannot allow you
to develop, you must be a photograph not a poem. You
must be rid of life as I am rid of life. We shall sink together
you and I, down, down into the dark voids where once
the vital organs were.

I have always admired your head. The strong front of
your forehead and the long crown. Your skull is slightly
bulbous at the back, giving way to a deep drop at the
nape of the neck. I have abseiled your head without fear.
I have held your head in my hands, taken it, soothed the
resistance, and held back my desire to probe under the skin

to the seat of you. In that hollow is where you exist. There the world is made and identified according to your omnivorous taxonomy. It's a strange combination of mortality and swank, the all-seeing, all-knowing brain, mistress of so much, capable of tricks and feats. Spoon-bending and higher mathematics. The hard-bounded space hides the vulnerable self.

I can't enter you in clothes that won't show the stains, my hands full of tools to record and analyse. If I come to you with a torch and a notebook, a medical diagram and a cloth to mop up the mess, I'll have you bagged neat and tidy. I'll store you in plastic like chicken livers. Womb, gut, brain, neatly labelled and returned. Is that how to know another human being?

I know how your hair tumbles from its chignon and washes your shoulders in light. I know the calcium of your cheekbones. I know the weapon of your jaw. I have held your head in my hands but I have never held you. Not you in your spaces, spirit, electrons of life.

'Explore me,' you said and I collected my ropes, flasks and maps, expecting to be back home soon. I dropped into the mass of you and I cannot find the way out. Sometimes I think I'm free, coughed up like Jonah from the whale, but then I turn a corner and recognise myself again. Myself in your skin, myself lodged in your bones, myself floating in the cavities that decorate every surgeon's wall. That is how I know you. You are what I know.

The Skin

THE SKIN IS COMPOSED OF TWO MAIN PARTS: THE DERMIS AND THE EPIDERMIS.

Odd to think that the piece of you I know best is already dead. The cells on the surface of your skin are thin and flat without blood vessels or nerve endings. Dead cells, thickest on the palms of your hands and the soles of your feet. Your sepulchral body, offered to me in the past tense, protects your soft centre from the intrusions of the outside world. I am one such intrusion, stroking you with necrophiliac obsession, loving the shell laid out before me.

The dead you is constantly being rubbed away by the dead me. Your cells fall and flake away, fodder to dust mites and bed bugs. Your droppings support colonies of life that graze on skin and hair no longer wanted. You don't feel a thing. How could you? All your sensation comes from deeper down, the live places where the dermis is renewing itself, making another armadillo layer. You are a knight in shining armour.

Rescue me. Swing me up beside you, let me hold on to you, arms around your waist, head nodding against your back. Your smell soothes me to sleep, I can bury myself in the warm goosedown of your body. Your skin tastes salty and slightly citrus. When I run my tongue in a long wet line across your breasts I can feel the tiny hairs, the puckering of the aureole, the cone of your nipple. Your breasts are beehives pouring honey.

I am a creature who feeds at your hand. I would be the squire rendering excellent service. Rest now, let me unlace your boots, massage your feet where the skin is calloused and sore. There is nothing distasteful about you to me; not sweat nor grime, not disease and its dull markings. Put your foot in my lap and I will cut your nails and ease the tightness of a long day. It has been a long day for you to find me. You are bruised all over. Burst figs are the livid purple of your skin.

The leukaemic body hurts easily. I could not be rough with you now, making you cry out with pleasure close to pain. We've bruised each other, broken the capillaries shot with blood. Tubes hair-thin intervening between arteries and veins, those ramified blood vessels that write the body's longing. You used to flush with desire. That was when we were in control, our bodies conspirators in our pleasure.

My nerve endings became sensitive to minute changes in your skin temperature. No longer the crude lever of Hot or Cold, I tried to find the second when your skin thickened. The beginning of passion, heat coming through, heartbeat deepening, quickening. I knew your blood vessels were swelling and your pores expanding. The physiological effects of lust are easy to read. Sometimes you sneezed four or five times like a cat. It's such an ordinary thing, happening millions of times a day all over the world. An ordinary miracle, your body changing under my hands. And yet, how to believe in the obvious surprise? Extraordinary, unlikely that you should want me.

I'm living on my memories like a cheap has-been. I've been sitting in this chair by the fire, my hand on the cat, talking aloud, fool-ramblings. There's a doctor's text-book fallen open on the floor. To me it's a book of spells. Skin, it says. Skin.

You were milk-white and fresh to drink. Will your skin discolour, its brightness blurring? Will your neck and spleen distend? Will the rigorous contours of your stomach swell under an infertile load? It may be so and the private drawing I keep of you will be a poor reproduction then. It may be so but if you are broken then so am I.

The Skeleton

THE CLAVICLE OR COLLAR BONE: THE CLAVICLE IS A LONG
BONE WHICH HAS A DOUBLE CURVE. THE SHAFT OF THE BONE
IS ROUGHENED FOR THE ATTACHMENT OF THE MUSCLES. THE
CLAVICLE PROVIDES THE ONLY BONY LINK BETWEEN THE
UPPER EXTREMITY AND THE AXIAL SKELETON.

I cannot think of the double curve lithe and flowing
with movement as a bony ridge, I think of it as the
musical instrument that bears the same root. Clavis.
Key. Clavichord. The first stringed instrument with a
keyboard. Your clavicle is both keyboard and key. If I
push my fingers into the recesses behind the bone I find
you like a soft shell crab. I find the openings between the
springs of muscle where I can press myself into the chords
of your neck. The bone runs in perfect scale from sternum
to scapula. It feels lathe-turned. Why should a bone be
balletic?

You have a dress with a décolletage to emphasise your
breasts. I suppose the cleavage is the proper focus but what
I wanted to do was to fasten my index finger and thumb at
the bolts of your collar bone, push out, spreading the web
of my hand until it caught against your throat. You asked
me if I wanted to strangle you. No, I wanted to fit you,
not just in the obvious ways but in so many indentations.

It was a game, fitting bone on bone. I thought difference was rated to be the largest part of sexual attraction
but there are so many things about us that are the same.

Bone of my bone. Flesh of my flesh. To remember

you it's my own body I touch. Thus she was, here and here. The physical memory blunders through the doors the mind has tried to seal. A skeleton key to Bluebeard's chamber. The bloody key that unlocks pain. Wisdom says forget, the body howls. The bolts of your collar bone undo me. Thus she was, here and here.

THE SCAPULA OR SHOULDER BLADE: THE SCAPULA IS A FLAT TRIANGULAR SHAPED BONE WHICH LIES ON THE POSTERIOR WALL SUPERFICIAL TO THE RIBS AND SEPARATED FROM THEM BY MUSCLE.

Shuttered like a fan no-one suspects your shoulder blades of wings. While you lay on your belly I kneaded the hard edges of your flight. You are a fallen angel but still as the angels are; body light as a dragonfly, great gold wings cut across the sun.

If I'm not careful you'll cut me. If I slip my hand too casually down the sharp side of your scapula I will lift away a bleeding palm. I know the stigmata of presumption. The wound that will not heal if I take you for granted.

Nail me to you. I will ride you like a nightmare. You are the winged horse Pegasus who would not be saddled. Strain under me. I want to see your muscle skein flex and stretch. Such innocent triangles holding hidden strength. Don't rear at me with unfolding power. I fear you in our bed when I put out my hand to touch you and feel the twin razors turned towards me. You sleep with your back towards me so that I will know the full extent of you. It is sufficient.

THE FACE: THERE ARE THIRTEEN BONES THAT FORM THE SKEL-
ETON OF THE FACE. FOR COMPLETENESS THE FRONTAL BONE
SHOULD BE ADDED.

Of the visions that come to me waking and sleeping the
most insistent is your face. Your face, mirror-smooth and
mirror-clear. Your face under the moon, silvered with cool
reflection, your face in its mystery, revealing me.

I cut out your face where it had caught in the ice on the
pond, your face bigger than my body, your mouth filled
with water. I held you against my chest on that snowy day,
the outline of you jagged into my jacket. When I put my
lips to your frozen cheek you burned me. The skin tore at
the corner of my mouth, my mouth filled with blood. The
closer I held you to me, the faster you melted away. I held
you as Death will hold you. Death that slowly pulls down
the skin's heavy curtain to expose the bony cage behind.

The skin loosens, yellows like limestone, like limestone worn by time, shows up the marbling of veins.
The pale translucency hardens and grows cold. The bones
themselves yellow into tusks.

Your face gores me. I am run through. Into the holes I
pack splinters of hope but hope does not heal me. Should
I pad my eyes with forgetfulness, eyes grown thin through
looking? Frontal bone, palatine bones, nasal bones, lacri-
mal bones, cheek bones, maxilla, vomer, inferior conchae,
mandible.

Those are my shields, those are my blankets, those
words don't remind me of your face.

The Special Senses

HEARING AND THE EAR: THE AURICLE IS THE EXPANDED POR-
TION WHICH PROJECTS FROM THE SIDE OF THE HEAD. IT IS
COMPOSED OF FIBRO-ELASTIC CARTILAGE COVERED WITH SKIN
AND FINE HAIRS. IT IS DEEPLY GROOVED AND RIDGED. THE
PROMINENT OUTER RIDGE IS KNOWN AS THE HELIX. THE LOB-
ULE IS THE SOFT PLIABLE PART AT THE LOWER EXTREMITY.

Sound waves travel at about 335 metres a second. That's
about a fifth of a mile and Louise is perhaps two hundred
miles away. If I shout now, she'll hear me in seventeen
minutes or so. I have to leave a margin of error for the
unexpected. She may be swimming under water.

I call Louise from the doorstep because I know she
can't hear me. I keen in the fields to the moon. Animals
in the zoo do the same, hoping that another of their kind
will call back. The zoo at night is the saddest place. Behind
the bars, at rest from vivisecting eyes, the animals cry out,
species separated from one another, knowing instinctive-
ly the map of belonging. They would choose predator
and prey against this outlandish safety. Their ears, more
powerful than those of their keepers, pick up sounds of
cars and last-hour take-aways. They hear all the human
noises of distress. What they don't hear is the hum of the
undergrowth or the crack of fire. The noises of kill. The
river-roar booming against brief screams. They prick their
ears till their ears are sharp points but the noises they seek
are too far away.

I wish I could hear your voice again.

THE NOSE: THE SENSE OF SMELL IN HUMAN BEINGS IS GEN-
ERALLY LESS ACUTE THAN IN OTHER ANIMALS.

The smells of my lover's body are still strong in my
nostrils. The yeast smell of her sex. The rich ferment-
ing undertow of rising bread. My lover is a kitchen cooking partridge. I shall visit her gamey low-roofed den and
feed from her. Three days without washing and she is
well-hung and high. Her skirts reel back from her body,
her scent is a hoop about her thighs.

From beyond the front door my nose is twitching, I
can smell her coming down the hall towards me. She is
a perfumier of sandalwood and hops. I want to uncork
her. I want to push my head against the open wall of her
loins. She is firm and ripe, a dark compound of sweet cattle
straw and Madonna of the Incense. She is frankincense and
myrrh, bitter cousin smells of death and faith.

When she bleeds the smells I know change colour.
There is iron in her soul on those days. She smells like a
gun.

My lover is cocked and ready to fire. She has the
scent of her prey on her. She consumes me when she
comes in thin white smoke smelling of saltpetre. Shot
against her all I want are the last wreaths of her desire
that carry from the base of her to what doctors like to
call the olfactory nerves.

TASTE: THERE ARE FOUR FUNDAMENTAL SENSATIONS OF
TASTE: SWEET SOUR BITTER AND SALT.

My lover is an olive tree whose roots grow by the sea.
Her fruit is pungent and green. It is my joy to get at the
stone of her. The little stone of her hard by the tongue.
Her thick-fleshed salt-veined swaddle stone.

Who eats an olive without first puncturing the swaddle? The waited moment when the teeth shoot a strong
burst of clear juice that has in it the weight of the land,
the vicissitudes of the weather, even the first name of the
olive keeper.

The sun is in your mouth. The burst of an olive is
breaking of a bright sky. The hot days when the rains
come. Eat the day where the sand burned the soles of
your feet before the thunderstorm brought up your skin
in bubbles of rain.

Our private grove is heavy with fruit. I shall worm
you to the stone, the rough swaddle stone.

THE EYE: THE EYE IS SITUATED IN THE ORBITAL CAVITY. IT
IS ALMOST SPHERICAL IN SHAPE AND ABOUT ONE INCH IN
DIAMETER.

Light travels at 186,000 miles per second. Light is
reflected into the eyes by whatever comes within the field
of vision. I see colour when a wavelength of light is
reflected by an object and all other wavelengths are
absorbed. Every colour has a different wavelength; red
light has the longest.

Is that why I seem to see it everywhere? I am living
in a red bubble made up of Louise's hair. It's the sunset
time of year but it's not the dropping disc of light that
holds me in the shadows of the yard. It's the colour I
crave, floodings of you running down the edges of the
sky on to the brown earth on to the grey stone. On to
me.

Sometimes I run into the sunset arms wide like a
scarecrow, thinking I can jump off the side of the world
into the fiery furnace and be burned up in you. I would
like to wrap my body in the blazing streaks of bloodshot
sky.

All other colours are absorbed. The dull tinges of
the day never penetrate my blackened skull. I live in
four blank walls like an anchorite. You were a brightly
lit room and I shut the door. You were a coat of many
colours wrestled into the dirt.

Do you see me in my blood-soaked world? Green-eyed girl, eyes wide apart like almonds, come in tongues of flame and restore my sight.

March. Elgin had promised to write to me in March.

I counted the days like someone under house arrest. It was bitter cold and the woods were filled with wild white daffodils. I tried to take comfort from the flowers, from the steady budding of the trees. This was new life, surely some of it would rub off on me?

The wine bar, otherwise known as 'A Touch of Southern Comfort', was staging a spring festival to attract back customers whose overdrafts still hadn't recovered from the Christmas festival. For us who worked there, this meant dressing in lime-green body stockings with a simple crown of artificial crocuses about our heads. The drinks had a spring theme: March Hare Punch, Wild Oat Sling, Blue Tit. It didn't matter what you ordered, the ingredients were the same apart from the liquor base. I mixed cheap cooking brandy, Japanese whisky, something that called itself gin and the occasional filthy sherry with pulp orange juice, thin cream, cubes of white sugar and various kitchen colourings. Soda water to top up and at £5.00 a couple (we only served couples at Southern Comfort) cheap at the price during Happy Hour.

The management ordered a March pianist and told him to make his way at his own speed through the Simon and Garfunkel songbook. For some reason he became autistically stuck at 'Bridge Over Troubled Water'. Whenever I arrived for work at 5 o'clock the silver girl was sailing by on words supplied by a tearful crowd of already tipsy punters. Against the lush chords and the aching tremeloes of our guests, we Spring Greens leapt from table to table, dropping food parcels of pizza and jugs of consolation. I began to despise my fellow man.

Still no word from Elgin. Work harder, mix more cocktails, stay up late, don't sleep, don't think. I might have taken to the bottle had there been anything fit to drink.

'I'd like to see where you live.'

I was behind the bar grimly jigging a few pints of Lethal Extra when Gail Right made it clear that she was coming home with me. At two in the morning when the last of our night birds had been tipped from their sodden nest, she locked up and put my push bike in the hatch of her car. She had a Tammy Wynette tape on the cassette.

'You're very reserved,' she said. 'I like that. I don't get a lot of it at work.'

'Why do you run that place?'

'I have to do something for a living. Can't depend on Prince Charming at my age.' She laughed. 'Or with my tastes.'

Stand by your man, said Tammy, and show the world you love him.

'I'm thinking of having a Country and Western Festival in the summer, what about it?' Gail was taking the corners too fast.

'What will we have to wear?'

She laughed again, more shrilly this time. 'Don't you like your little body stocking? I think you look gorgeous.' She pronounced the word with an accented 'O' so that it sounded less like a compliment and more like the gaping chasm.

'It's very good of you to drop me off,' I said. 'I can offer you something if you like.'

'Ooh yes,' she said. 'Ooh yes.'

We got out of her car under the frozen sky. I unlocked my door with frozen fingers and invited her in with a frozen heart.

'Lovely and warm in here,' she said snuggling herself

in front of the stove. She had a vast bottom. It reminded me of a pair of shorts a boyfriend of mine had once worn which said (GL)ASS. HANDLE WITH CARE. She wiggled and knocked over a Toby jug.

'Don't worry,' I said. 'It was too fat for the fireplace.'

She eased herself into the trembling armchair and accepted my offering of cocoa with a leer about Casanova. I had thought that was an esoteric fact.

'It's not true,' I said. 'Chocolate is a wonderful sedative.' Which isn't true either but I thought Gail Right might be susceptible to a bit of Mind over Matter. I yawned pointedly.

'Busy day,' she said. 'Busy day. Makes me think of other things. Dark exciting things.'

I thought of treacle. What would it be like to be caught in the wallow of Gail Right?

I had a boyfriend once, his name was Carlo, he was a dark exciting thing. He made me shave off all my body hair and did the same to himself. He claimed it would increase sensation but it made me feel like a prisoner in a beehive. I wanted to please him, he smelled of fir cones and port, his long body passion–damp. We lasted six months and then Carlo met Robert who was taller, broader and thinner than me. They exchanged razorblades and cut me out.

'What are you dreaming about?' asked Gail.

'An old love.'

'You like 'em old do you? That's good. Mind you, I'm not as old as I look, not when you get down to the upholstery.'

She gave the armchair a mighty thwack and a cloud of dust settled over her exhausted make-up.

'I have to tell you now Gail that there's someone else.'

'There always is,' she sighed and stared into the murky lumps of her cocoa like a fortune teller on a fix. 'Tall, dark, and handsome?'

'Tall, red and beautiful.'

'Give us a bedtime story then,' said Gail. 'What's she like?'

Louise, dipterous girl born in flames, 35. 34 22 36. 10 years married. 5 months with me. Doctorate in Art History. First class mind. 1 miscarriage (or 2?) 0 children. 2 arms, 2 legs, too many white T-cells. 97 months to live.

'Don't cry,' said Gail, kneeling in front of my chair, her plump ringed hand on my thin empty ones. 'Don't cry. You did the right thing. She would have died, how could you have forgiven yourself that? You've given her a chance.'

'It's incurable.'

'That's not what her doctor says. She can trust him, can't she?'

I hadn't told Gail everything.

She touched my face very softly. 'You'll be happy again. We could be happy together couldn't we?'

Six in the morning and I was lying in my saggy rented double bed with Gail Right sagging beside me. She smelled of face powder and dry rot. She was snoring heavily and would be for some time to come, so I got up, borrowed her car, and drove to the phone box.

We hadn't made love. I'd run my hands over her padded flesh with all the enthusiasm of a second-hand sofa dealer. She'd patted my head and fallen asleep, which was as well since my body had all the sensitivity of a wet-suit.

I put the money in the slot and listened to the ringing tones while my breath steamed up the barren phone box.

My heart was over-beating. Someone answered, sleepy, grumpy.

'HELLO? HELLO?'

'Hello Elgin.'

'What time do you call this?'

'Early morning after another sleepless night.'

'What do you want?'

'Our agreement. How is she?'

'Louise is in Switzerland. She's been quite ill but she's much better now. We have had good results. She won't be back in England for some time if at all. You can't see her.'

'I don't want to see her.' (LIAR LIAR.)

'That's good because she certainly doesn't want to see you.'

The phone went dead. I held on to the receiver for a moment, staring stupidly into the mouthpiece. Louise was OK, that was all that mattered.

I got into the car and drove the deserted miles home. Sunday morning and no-one around. The upstairs rooms were tightly curtained, the houses on the road were still asleep. A fox ran across my path, a chicken hanging limply from its mouth. I would have to deal with Gail.

At home there were only two sounds: the metallic ticking of the clock and Gail's snores. I closed the door on the stairs and left myself alone with the clock. In the very early morning the hours have a different quality, they stretch and promise. I took out my books and tried to work. Russian is the only language I'm good at, which is a help since there aren't that many of us competing for the same jobs. The Francophiles have a terrible time, everybody wants to sit outside a Paris café and translate the new edition of Proust. Not me. I used to think that a tour de force was a school trip.

'You idiot,' said Louise cuffing me gently.

She got up to make coffee and brought it in fresh with the smell of plantations and sun. The aromatic steam warmed our faces and clouded my glasses. She drew a heart on each lens. 'So that you won't see anybody but me,' she said. Her hair cinnabar red, her body all the treasures of Egypt. There won't be another find like you Louise. I won't see anybody else.

I worked until the clock chimed twelve and there was a horrible heaving from upstairs. Gail Right had woken up.

I moved quickly to the kettle, sensing that some appeasement would be necessary. Would a mug of tea protect me? I put out my hand to Earl Grey and settled on Empire Blend. The Stand Up And Be Counted of teas. A man-sized tea. A tea with so much tannin that designers use it as pigment.

She was in the bathroom. I heard the judder judder of the water pipes then the assault against the enamel. Unwillingly the tank was forced to part with every drop of hot water, it wheezed to the very end then came to a stop with a dreadful clank. I hoped she hadn't disturbed the sediment.

'Never disturb the Sediment,' the farmer had said when he'd showed me round the place. He said it as though the Sediment were some fearful creature who lived under the hot water.

'What will happen if I do?'

He shook his head doomfully. 'Can't say.'

I'm sure he meant he didn't know but did he have to make it sound like an ancient curse?

I took Gail her tea and knocked at the door.

'Don't be shy,' she called.

I prised open the door from its stiff catch and plonked the tea on the bathside. The water was brown. Gail was streaky. She looked like a prime cut of streaky bacon. Her eyes were small and red from the night before. Her hair stuck out like a straw rick. I shuddered.

'Cold isn't it?' she said. 'Scrub my back honey will you?'

'Must stoke up the fire, Gail. Can't let you get cold.'

I fled down the stairs and did indeed stoke up the fire. I would gladly have stoked the whole house and left it roasting Gail inside. This isn't polite, I told myself. Why are you so horror-struck by a woman whose only fault is to like you and whose only quality is to be larger than life?

Bam, Bam, Bam, Bam, Bam, Bam, Bam. Gail Right was at the bottom of the stairs. I straightened up and made a quick smile.

'Hello love,' she said kissing me with a suckering sound. 'Got any bacon sandwiches?'

While Gail made her way through what was left of Autumn Effie, the farmer's yearly pig to the slaughter, she told me she was going to change my shifts at the wine bar so that we could work together. 'I'll give you more money as well.' She licked the grease from her lower lip and where it had dripped on to her arm.

'I'd rather not. I like things the way they are.'

'You're in shock. Try it my way for a bit.' She leered at me over the crusts of her breakfast. 'Didn't you enjoy a bit of home company last night? Those hands of yours got everywhere.'

Her own hands were wedging Effie between her jaws as though she feared the pig might still have the guts to make a break for it. She had fried the bacon herself then soaked the bread in the fat before shutting the sandwich. Her fingernails were not quite free of red polish and some of this had found its way on to the bread.

'I love a bacon sandwich,' she said. 'The way you touched me. So light and nimble, do you play the piano?'

'Yes,' I said in an unnaturally high voice. 'Excuse me please.'

I got to the toilet just ahead of my vomit. On your knees, seat up head down, stucco the bowl with porridge. I wiped my mouth and rinsed out with water, spitting away the burning in the back of my throat. If Louise had had chemotherapy she might be suffering this every morning. And I wasn't with her. 'Remember that's the point, that's the point,' I said to myself in the mirror. 'That's the route she won't have to take so long as she's with Elgin.'

'How do you know?' said the piping doubting voice I had come so much to fear.

I crept back into the sitting room and took a swig of whisky from the bottle. Gail was doing her make-up in a pocket mirror. 'Not a vice I hope?' she said squinting under her eyeliner.

'I'm not feeling well.'

'You don't get enough sleep, that's your trouble. I heard you at six o'clock this morning. Where did you go?'

'I had to telephone someone.'

Gail put down her wand of mascara. It said wand on the side of the tube but it looked more like a cowprod.

'You've got to forget her.'

'I may as well forget myself.'

'What shall we do today?'

'I've got to work.'

Gail considered me for a moment then bundled her

tools in their vinyl bag. 'You're not interested in me honey are you?'

'It's not that I . . . '

'I know, you think I'm a fat old slag who just wants a piece of something firm and juicy. Well you're right. But I'd do my share of the work. I'd care for you and be a good friend to you and see you right. I'm not a sponger, I'm not a tart. I'm a good-time girl whose body has blown. Shall I tell you something honey? You don't lose your lust at the rate you lose your looks. It's a cruel fact of nature. You go on fancying it just the same. And that's hard but I've got a few things left. I don't come to the table empty handed.'

She got up and took her keys. 'Think about it. You know where to find me.'

I watched her drive off in her car and I felt depressed and ashamed. I went back to bed, gave up the fight and dreamed of Louise.

April. May. I continued my training as a cancer specialist. They got to call me the Hospital Ghoul down at the Terminal Ward. I didn't care. I visited patients, listened to their stories, found ones who'd got well and sat by ones who died. I thought all cancer patients would have strong loving families. The research hype is about going through it together. It's almost a family disease. The truth is that many cancer patients die alone.

'What do you want?' one of the junior doctors finally asked me.

'I want to know what it's like. I want to know what it is.'

She shrugged. 'You're wasting your time. Most days I think we're all wasting our time.'

'Then why bother? Why do you bother?'

'Why bother? That's a question for the whole human

race isn't it?'

She turned to go and then turned back to me worried.

'You haven't got cancer have you?'

'No!'

She nodded. 'You see, sometimes people who have been newly diagnosed want the inside story on the treatment. Doctors are very patronising, even to highly intelligent patients. Some of those patients like to find out for themselves.'

'What do they find out?'

'How little we know. It's the late twentieth century and what are the tools of our trade? Knives, saws, needles and chemicals. I've no time for alternative medicine but I can see why it's attractive.'

'Shouldn't you have time for any possibility?'

'On an eighty-hour shift?'

She left. I took my book, *The Modern Management of Cancer*, and went home.

June. The driest June on record. The earth that should have been in summer glory was thin for lack of water. The buds held promise but they didn't swell. The beating sun was a fake. The sun that should have brought life was carrying death in every relentless morning.

I decided to go to church. Not because I wanted to be saved, nor because I wanted solace from the cross. Rather, I wanted the comfort of other people's faith. I like to be anonymous among the hymn-singing crowd, the stranger at the door who doesn't have to worry about the fund for the roof or the harvest festival display. It used to be that everybody believed and faith was found in thousands of tiny churches up and down the British Isles. I miss the Sunday morning bells ringing from village to village.

God's jungle telegraph bearing the good news. And it was good news insomuch as the church was a centre and a means. The Church of England in its unexcited benevolent concern was emphatically to do with village life. The slow moving of the seasons, the corresponding echo in the *Book of Common Prayer*. Ritual and silence. Rough stone and rough soil. Now, it's hard to find one church in four that still runs a full calendar and is something more than a bit of communion every other Sunday and the odd parish event.

The church not far from me was a working model not a museum so I chose evensong and polished my shoes. I should have known there'd be a catch.

The building was thirteenth-century in parts with Georgian and Victorian repairs. It was of the solid stone that seems to rise organically from the land itself. Grown not made. The colour and substance of battle. The battle to hew it out and shape it for God. It was massy, soil-black and defiant. Across the architrave of the low front door was a plastic banner which said JESUS LOVES YOU.

'Move with the times,' I said to myself, slightly uneasy.

I walked inside across the cool flagged floor, the particular church cold that no amount of gas fires and overcoats can penetrate. After the heat of the day it felt like the hand of God. I slid into a dark pew with a tree on the door and looked for my prayer book. There wasn't one. Then the tambourines started. These were serious tambourines the size of bass drums, flaunting ribbons like a Maypole and studded round the side like the collar of a pitbull. One came down the aisle towards me and flashed at my ear. 'Praise the Lord,' said its owner, desperately trying to keep it under control. 'A stranger in our midst.'

The entire congregation except for me then broke

into a melody of Bible texts and scattered shouts liberally set to music. The magnificent pipe organ stood shuttered and dusty, we had an accordion and two guitars. I really wanted to get out but there was a burly beaming farmer standing across the main door who looked as though he might get nasty if I ran for it before the collection.

'Jesus will overcome you,' cried the minister. (God the wrestler?)

'Jesus will have his way with you!' (God the rapist?)

'Jesus is going from strength to strength!' (God the body builder?)

'Hand yourself over to Jesus and you will be returned with interest.'

I am prepared to accept the many-sidedness of God but I am sure that if God exists He is not a Building Society.

I had a boyfriend once, his name was Bruno. After forty years of dissolution and Mammon he found Jesus under a wardrobe. In fairness, the wardrobe had been slowly crushing the resistance from his lungs for about four hours. He did house clearances and had fallen foul of a double-doored Victorian loomer. The sort of wardrobe poor people lived in. He was eventually rescued by the fire brigade though he always maintained it was the Lord himself who had levitated the oak ever upwards. He took me to church with him soon after and gave a graphic account of how Jesus had come out of the closet to save him. 'Out of the closet and up into your heart,' raved the Pastor.

I never saw Bruno after that, he gave me his motorbike as a gesture of renouncement and prayed that it might lead me to the Lord. Sadly it blew up on the outskirts of Brighton.

Ripping through this harmless reverie, a pair of hands seized mine and started banging them together as if they were cymbals. I realised I was meant to be clapping in time to the beat and I remembered another piece of advice from my grandmother. 'When in the jungle you howl with the wolves.' I slapped a plastic grin on my face like a server at McDonald's and pretended to be having a good time. I wasn't having a bad time, I wasn't having any time at all. No wonder they talk about Jesus filling a vacuum as though human beings were thermos flasks. This was the most vacuous place I'd ever been. God may be compassionate but he must have some taste.

As I suspected, the sumo farmer was in charge of the collection, so as soon as he had joyfully collected my bent twenty pence piece, I fled. I fled into the raw fields where the sheep continued their grazing as they had done for ten centuries. I fled to the pond where the dragonflies fed. I fled till the church was a hard knot against the sky. If prayer is appropriate it was appropriate here, my back against a dry stone wall, my feet on the slabbed earth. I had prayed for Louise every day since December. I did not know entirely to whom I prayed or even why. But I wanted someone to have care of her. To visit her and comfort her. To be the cool wind and the deep stream. I wanted her to be protected and I would have boiled cauldrons of stuffed newts if I'd been convinced it would have done any good. As to prayer, it helped me to concentrate my mind. To think of Louise in her own right, not as my lover, not as my grief. It helped me to forget myself and that was a great blessing. 'You made a mistake,' said the voice. The voice wasn't a piping sly voice now it was a strong gentle voice and I heard it quite clearly more and more. I did hear it out loud and I was not sure that my wits were still mine to command. What kind of people hear voices? Joan of Arc yes but what about all the others, the sad or sinister ones who want to change the world by tambourine power.

I hadn't been able to reach Elgin this month although I had written to him three times and telephoned him at every hour proper and improper. I supposed him to be in Switzerland but what if Louise were dying? Would he tell me? Would he let me see her again? I shook my head. That would be wrong. That would make a nonsense of all of this. Louise wasn't dying, she was safe in Switzerland. She was standing in a long green skirt by the drop of a torrent. The waterfall ran down from her hair over her breasts, her skirt was transparent. I looked more closely. Her body was transparent. I saw the course of her blood, the ventricles of her heart, her legs' long bones like tusks. Her blood was clean and red like summer roses. She was fragrant and in bud. No drought. No pain. If Louise is well then I am well.

I found one of her hairs on a coat of mine today. The gold streak caught the light. I bound it around my forefingers and pulled it straight. It was nearly two feet long that way. Is this the thread that binds me to you?

No-one tells you in grief-counselling or books on loss what it will be like when you find part of the beloved unexpectedly. The wisdom is to make sure your house is not a mausoleum, only to keep those things that bring you happy positive memories. I had been reading books that dealt with death partly because my separation from Louise was final and partly because I knew she would die and that I would have to cope with this second loss, perhaps just as the first was less inflamed. I wanted to cope.

Although I felt that my life had been struck in two I still wanted life. I have never thought of suicide as a solution to unhappiness.

Some years ago a friend of mine was killed in a road accident. She was crushed to death on her bicycle under the sixteen wheels of a juggernaut.

When I recovered from her death in the crudest sense I started to see her in the streets, always fleetingly, ahead of me, her back to me, disappearing into the crowd. I am told this is common. I see her still, though less often, and still for a second I believe it is her. I have from time to time found something of hers among my possessions. Always something trivial. Once I opened an old notebook and a slip of paper fell out, pristine, the ink firm not faded. She had left it at my seat in the British Library five years earlier. It was an invitation to coffee at four o'clock. I'll get my coat and a handful of small change and meet you in the crowded cafe and you'll be there today won't you, won't you?

'You'll get over it . . . ' It's the clichés that cause the trouble. To lose someone you love is to alter your life for ever. You don't get over it because 'it' is the person you loved. The pain stops, there are new people, but the gap never closes. How could it? The particularness of someone who mattered enough to grieve over is not made anodyne by death. This hole in my heart is in the shape of you and no-one else can fit it. Why would I want them to?

I've thought a lot about death recently, the finality of it, the argument ending in mid-air. One of us hadn't finished, why did the other one go? And why without warning? Even death after long illness is without warning. The moment you had prepared for so carefully took you by storm. The troops broke through the window and snatched the body and the body is gone. The day before the Wednesday last, this time a year ago, you were here and now you're not. Why not? Death reduces us to the baffled logic of a small child. If yesterday why not today? And where are you?

Fragile creatures of a small blue planet, surrounded by light years of silent space. Do the dead find peace beyond the rattle of the world? What peace is there for us whose best love cannot return them even for a day? I raise my head to the door and think I will see you in the frame. I know it is your voice in the corridor but when I run outside the corridor is empty. There is nothing I can do that will make any difference. The last word was yours.

The fluttering in the stomach goes away and the dull waking pain. Sometimes I think of you and I feel giddy. Memory makes me lightheaded, drunk on champagne. All the things we did. And if anyone had said this was the price I would have agreed to pay it. That surprises me; that with the hurt and the mess comes a shaft of recognition. It was worth it. Love is worth it.

August. Nothing to report. For the first time since leaving Louise I was depressed. The previous months had been wild with despair and cushioned by shock. I had been half mad, if madness is to be on the fringes of the real world. In August I felt blank and sick. I had sobered up, come round to the facts of what I had done. I was no longer drunk on grief. Body and mind know how to hide from what is too sore to handle. Just as the burns victim reaches a plateau of pain, so do the emotionally wretched find grief is a high ground from which they may survey themselves for a time. Such detachment was no longer mine. I was drained of my manic energy and also of my tears. I fell into dead sleeps and woke unrested. When my heart hurt I could no longer cry. There was only the weight of wrong-doing. I had failed Louise and it was too late.

What right had I to decide how she should live? What right had I to decide how she should die?

At A Touch of Southern Comfort it was Country and Western Month. It was also Gail Right's birthday. Not surprisingly she was a Leo. On the night in question, hot beyond hell and loud beyond decibels, we were celebrating at the feet of Howlin' Dog House Don. HD² as he liked to be called. The fringes on his jacket would have made a whole head of hair had he needed it. He did need it but he believed his Invisible Toupee was just that. His trousers were tight enough to choke a weasel. When he wasn't singing into his microphone he cradled it against his crotch. He wore a NO ENTRY sign over his bum.

'Cheek,' said Gail and roared at her own pun. 'I've seen better colons on a typewriter.'

HD² was a big hit. The women loved the way he threw them red paper hankies from his top pocket and growled into the bass notes like a gravelly Elvis. The men didn't seem too worried by his bum jokes. He sat on their knees and squawked, 'Who's a pretty boy then?' while the women anchored themselves round another gin and lime.

'I'm doin' a Hen Night next week,' said Gail. 'Strip tease.'

'I thought this was Country and Western?'

'It is. He's gonna wear a bandanna.'

'What about the banana? Doesn't look much from here.'

'It's not the size they're after, it's the laugh.'

I looked at the stage. Howlin' Dog House Don was holding his microphone stand at arm's length and crooning, 'Is it really you oo oo?'

'Better get ready,' said Gail. 'When he's finished this one they'll be queueing at the bar faster than an outing of nuns at the true cross.'

She had mixed a washing-up bowl full of Dolly Parton on Ice, this month's special. I began to line up the glasses and the tiny plastic bosoms that were replacing our cocktail umbrellas.

'Come out for a meal after work,' said Gail. 'No strings. I'm finishing at midnight, I'll finish you too if you fancy it.'

That was how I ended up in front of a Spaghetti Carbonara at Magic Pete's.

Gail was drunk. She was so drunk that when her false eyelash fell into her soup she told the waiter it was a centipede.

'I got something to tell you kiddo,' she said leaning down at me the way a zoo keeper drops a fish at a penguin. 'Want it?'

There was nothing else to have. Magic Pete's was an all-night drinking club, low on amenity, high on booze. It was Gail's revelation or find 50p for the juke box. I didn't have 50p.

'You made a mistake.'

In cartoon land this is where a saw comes up through the floor and teeths a neat hole round Bugs Bunny's chair. What does she mean 'I made a mistake'?

'If you mean about us Gail, I couldn't . . . '

She interrupted me. 'I mean about you and Louise.'

She could hardly get the words out. She had her mouth propped on her fists and her elbows propped on the table. She kept trying to reach for my hand and falling sideways into the ice-bucket.

'You shouldn't have run out on her.'

Run out on her? That doesn't sound like the heroics I'd had in mind. Hadn't I sacrificed myself for her? Offered my life for her life?

'She wasn't a child.'

Yes she was. My child. My baby. The tender thing I wanted to protect.

'You didn't give her a chance to say what she wanted. You left.'

I had to leave. She would have died for my sake. Wasn't it better for me to live a half life for her sake?

'What's the matter?' slurred Gail. 'Cat got your tongue?'

Not the cat, the worm of doubt. Who do I think I am? Sir Launcelot? Louise is a Pre-Raphaelite beauty but that doesn't make me a mediaeval knight. Nevertheless I desperately wanted to be right.

We staggered out of Magic Pete's towards Gail's car. I wasn't drunk but supporting Gail was a staggering sort of business. She was like a left-over jelly at a children's party. She decided she was coming home with me even if I had to sleep in the armchair. Mile by mile she reviewed my mistakes. I began to wish that I'd done as I first intended and kept back some of my story. There was no stopping her now. She was a three-ton truck on a slope.

'Honey, if there's one thing I can't stand it's a hero without a cause. People like that just make trouble so that they can solve it.'

'Is that what you think of me?'

'I think you're a crazy fool. Maybe you didn't love her.'

This caused me to swing the wheel so violently that Gail's gift-box collection of Tammy Wynette tapes skidded over the back and decapitated her nodding dog. Gail was sick down her blouse.

'The trouble with you,' she said wiping herself, 'is that you want to live in a novel.'

'Rubbish. I never read novels. Except Russian ones.'

'They're the worst. This isn't War and Peace honey, it's Yorkshire.'

'You're drunk.'

'That's right I am. I'm fifty-three and I'm as wild as a Welshman with a leek up his arse. Fifty-three. Old slag Gail. What right has she to poke her nose into your shining armour? That's what you're thinking isn't it honey? I may not look much like a messenger from the gods but your girl isn't the only one who's got wings. I've got a pair of my own under here.' (She patted her armpits.) 'I've flown about a bit and picked up a few things and I'll give one of them to you for nothing. You don't run out on the woman you love. Especially you don't when you think it's for her own good.' She hiccuped violently and covered her skirt with half-digested clams. I gave her my handkerchief. Finally she said, 'You'd better go and find her.'

'I can't.'

'Who said?'

'I said. I gave my word. Even if I am wrong it's too late now. Would you want to see me if I'd left you in the lurch with a man you despise?'

'Yes,' said Gail and passed out.

The following morning I caught the train to London. The heat through the carriage window made me sleepy and I slid into a light doze where Louise's voice came to me as if under water. She was under water. We were in Oxford and she was swimming in the river, green on the sheen of her, pearl sheen of her body. We had lain down on the grass sun-scorched, grass turning hay, grass brittle on the baked clay, spear grass marking us in red weals. The sky was blue as in blue-eyed boy, not a wink of cloud, steady gaze, what a smile. A pre-war sky. Before the first world war there were days and days like this; long English meadows, insect hum, innocence and blue sky. Farm workers pitching the hay, women in waist aprons carrying pitchers of lemonade. Summers were hot, winters were snowy. It's a pretty story.

Now here am I making up my own memories of good times. When we were together the weather was better, the days were longer. Even the rain was warm. That's right, isn't it? Do you remember when . . . I can see Louise sitting cross-legged under the plum tree in the Oxford garden. The plums have the look of asps' heads in her hair. Her hair is still drying from the river, curling up round the plums. Against her copper hair the green leaves look like tarnish. My Lady of the Verdigris. Louise is one of the few women who might still be beautiful if she went mouldy.

On that day she was asking me whether I would be true to her and I replied, 'With all my heart.' Had I been true to her?

Let me not to the marriage of true minds
Admit impediments; love is not love
Which alters when it alteration finds
Or bends with the remover to remove.
Oh no it is an ever fixed mark
That looks on tempests and is never shaken
It is the star to every wandering bark
Whose worth's unknown altho' his highth be taken.

When I was young I loved this sonnet. I thought a wandering bark was a young dog, rather as in Dylan Thomas's *Portrait of the Artist as a Young Dog*.

I have been a wandering bark of unknown worth but I thought I was a safe ship for Louise. Then I threw her overboard.

'Will you be true to me?'

'With all my heart.'

I took her hand and put it underneath my T-shirt. She took my nipple and squeezed it between finger and thumb.

'And with all your flesh?'

'You're hurting me Louise.'

Passion is not well bred. Her fingers bit their spot. She would have bound me to her with ropes and had us lie face to face unable to move but move on each other, unable to feel but feel each other. She would have deprived us of all senses bar the sense of touch and smell. In a blind, deaf and dumb world we could conclude our passion infinitely. To end would be to begin again. Only she, only me. She was jealous but so was I. She was brute with love but so was I. We were patient enough to count the hairs on each other's heads, too impatient to get undressed. Neither of us had the upper hand, we wore matching wounds. She was my twin and I lost her. Skin is waterproof but my skin was not waterproof against Louise. She flooded me and she has not drained away. I am still wading through her, she beats upon my doors and threatens my innermost safety. I have no gondola at the gate and the tide is still rising. Swim for it, don't be afraid. I am afraid.

Is this her revenge? 'I will never let you go.'

I went straight to my flat. I didn't expect to find Louise there and yet there were signs of her occupation, some clothes, books, the coffee she liked. Sniffing the coffee told me that she hadn't been there for some time, the beans had gone stale and she would never permit that. I picked up a sweater of hers and buried my face in it. Very faintly, her perfume.

I was strangely elated to be in my own home. Why are human beings so contradictory? This was the site of sorrow and separation, a place of mourning, but with the sun coming through the windows and the garden full of roses I felt hopeful again. We had been happy here too and some of that happiness had soaked the walls and patterned the furniture.

I decided to dust. I've found before that ceaseless menial work calms the rat-cage of the mind. I had to stop worrying and speculating for long enough to make a sensible plan. I needed peace and peace was not a quality I had come to know.

It was while I was scrubbing away the last of Miss Havisham that I found some letters to Louise from the hospital where she had gone for a second opinion. The letters were of the mind that since Louise was still asymptomatic no treatment should be considered. There was some swelling of the lymphatic nodes but this had remained stable for six months. The consultant advised regular checks and a normal life. The three letters were dated after I had left. There was also a very impressive document from Elgin reminding Louise that he had been studying her case for two years and that in his humble opinion ('May I remind you Louise that it is I and not Mr Rand who is best qualified to make decisions in this uncertain field') she needed treatment. The address of his Swiss clinic was on the letterhead.

I telephoned. The receptionist didn't want to talk to me. There were no patients at the clinic. No, I couldn't speak to Mr Rosenthal.

I began to wonder if the receptionist was one of Inge's.

'May I speak to Mrs Rosenthal?' (how I hated having to say that).

'Mrs Rosenthal is not here any longer.'

'Then may I speak to the doctor?'

'*Mr* Rosenthal' (she underlined my faux pas) 'is not here either.'

'Do you expect him?'

She couldn't say. I slammed down the phone and sat on the floor.

All right. Nothing else for it. Louise's mother.

Louise's mother and grandmother lived together in Chelsea. They considered themselves to be Australian aristocracy, that is, they were descended from convicts. They had a small mews house from whose upper floors they could see the Buckingham Palace flagpole. Grandmother spent all of her time on the upper floors, noting when and when not, the Queen was in residence. Occasionally she broke off to spill food down her front. She had a steady hand but she liked to spill. It made work for her daughter.

Louise was rather fond of her grandmother. With a little twist to Dickens, she called her The Aged Pea, peas were what grandmother spilled the most. Her only comment on Louise's separation from Elgin had been 'Get the money.'

Mother was more complicated and in a very unaristocratic fashion worried about what people would say. When I announced myself at the entryphone she refused to let me in.

'I don't know where she is and it's no business of yours.'

'Mrs Fox, please open the door, please.'

There was silence. An Englishman's home is his castle, but an Australian's mews house is fair game. I banged on the door with both fists and shouted Mrs Fox's name as loudly as I could. Immediately opposite, two coiffured heads popped into the window like Punch and Judy in their box. The front door flew open. It wasn't Mrs Fox but The Aged Pea herself.

'Think you're on a kangaroo shoot or somethin'?'

'I'm looking for Louise.'

'Don't you come through these doors.' Mrs Fox appeared.

'Kitty, if we don't let this digger in, neighbours'll think we got either the bugs or the bailiffs.' The Pea eyed me suspiciously. 'You have the look of a thing from the Disinfectant Department.'

'Mother, we don't have a Disinfectant Department in England.'

'We don't? That explains a whole lot of smells.'

'Please, Mrs Fox, I won't be long.'

Reluctantly Mrs Fox stood back and I stepped on to the mat.

When there was a centimetre gap between me and the

door, Mrs Fox shut it and barred my further passage. I could feel the plastic letter-box cover on my spine.

'Get it over with then.'

'I'm looking for Louise. When did you last see her?'

'Ho ho,' said the Pea banging her stick. 'Don't play the Waltzing Matilda with me. What do you care? You walked out on her, now get lost.'

Mrs Fox said, 'I'm glad you're having nothing more to do with my daughter. You broke up her marriage.'

'I've no quarrel with that,' said Grandma.

'Mother, will you be quiet? Elgin is a great man.'

'Since when? You always said he was a little rat.'

'I did not say he was a little rat. I said he was rather small and that unfortunately he had the look of a, well, I said a . . .'

'Rat!' screamed the Pea banging her stick on the door just by my head. She should have been a knife thrower in the circus.

'Mrs Fox. I made a mistake. I should never have left Louise. I thought it was for her own good. I thought Elgin could make her well. I want to find her and take care of her.'

'It's too late,' said Mrs Fox. 'She told me she never wanted to see you again.'

'She's had a worse time than a toad on a runway,' said the Pea.

'Mother, go and sit down, you're getting tired,' said Mrs Fox supporting herself on the banister rail. 'I can deal with this.'

'Prettiest thing this side of Brisbane and look how she's been treated. You know, Louise is the spitting image of myself when younger. I had quite a figure then.'

It was hard to imagine Pea having any figure. She

was like a child's drawing of a snowman, just two circles plonked one on top of the other. For the first time I noticed her hair: it was serpentine in its rising twists, a living moving mass that escaped from its tight bands just as Louise's did. Louise had told me that Pea had been the undisputed Beauty Queen of Western Australia. She had had over one hundred proposals of marriage in the 1920s from bankers, prospectors, city men who unrolled maps of the new Australia they were going to build and said, 'Sweet darling all this is yours when you are mine.' Pea had married a sheep farmer and had six children. Her nearest neighbour had been a day's ride away. I saw her suddenly, dress to the floor, hands on her hips, the dirt track disappearing into the flat of the horizon. Nothing but flat and the bar of the sky measuring the distance. Miss Helen Louise, a burning bush in the dry land.

'What you starin' at digger?'

I shook my head. 'Mrs Fox, have you any idea where Louise has gone?'

'I know she's not in London, that's all. She may be abroad.'

'Got a packet out of the doctor. She left him as lean as a woodlouse in a plastics factory. Heh heh heh.'

'Mother, will you stop it?' Mrs Fox turned to me, 'I think you'd better leave now. I can't help you.'

Mrs Fox opened the door as her neighbours closed theirs.

'What did I tell you all?' said Pea. 'We're in disrepute.'

She turned in disgust and pegged down the hall on her stick.

'You know, don't you, that Elgin was to be in the civil list this year? Louise cost him that.'

'Don't be ridiculous,' I said. 'A happy marriage has

nothing to do with it.'

'Then why wasn't he?' She slammed the door and I heard her crying in the hall. Was it for her lost connection with the great and the good or was it for her daughter?

Evening. Couples out on the sweating streets hand in hand. From an upper window a reggae band with a long way to go. Restaurants were pushing the alfresco style, but a wicker chair on a dirty street with the buses grinding by isn't Venice. I watched the litter blow among the pizzas and raffia carafes. A vulpine waiter fixed his dicky bow in the cashier's mirror, slapped her bottom, put a peppermint on his red tongue and swaggered over to a group of under-age girls drinking Campari and soda. 'Would madams like a something to a eat?'

I caught the first bus regardless of its destination. What did it matter since I was no nearer to Louise? The city was suppurating. The bus driver wouldn't open the doors while the bus was moving. The air in there smelt of burger and chips. There was a fat woman in a sleeveless nylon frock sitting with her legs apart fanning herself with her shoe. Her make-up had slipped into ledges of grime.

'OPEN THE DOORS FUCKFACE,' she shouted.

'Fuck off,' said the driver without looking round. 'Can't you read the notice? Can't you read?'

The notice said DO NOT DISTRACT DRIVER WHILE BUS IS IN MOTION. We were stock still in a traffic jam at the time.

As the temperature mounted the man in front of me resorted to his mobile phone. Like all mobile phone users he had nothing urgent to say, he simply wanted to say it. He looked at us all to see if we were looking at him. When he finally said, 'Goo nye then my mate Kev,' I asked him very politely if I might borrow it for a moment and offered him a pound coin. He was reluctant to separate himself from such an essential part of his machismo but he agreed to punch in the number for me and hold the phone to my ear. After it had rung pointlessly a few times he said, 'That's out then,' pocketed my pound and hung his treasure back round his neck on a bulldog chain. There had been no answer at Louise's house. I decided to go and see for myself.

I found a cab to take me through the thick heat of the dying day and we turned into the square at the same moment as Elgin's BMW pulled up at the kerb. He got out and opened the passenger door for a woman. She was a little business suit number, serious make-up and the sort of hairdo that looks on tempests and is never shaken. She had a small travel bag, Elgin a suitcase, they were laughing together. He kissed her and fumbled for his keys.

'You gettin' out or not?' asked my driver.

I was trying to control myself. On the doorstep breathing deeply I rang the bell. Keep calm Keep calm Keep calm.

The hot date answered the door. I smiled brightly and walked around her into the wide hall. Elgin had his back to me.

'Darling . . . ' she began.

'Hello Elgin.'

He spun round. I didn't think people did that in real life, only in kooky crime thrillers. Elgin moved like Fred Astaire and placed himself between me and the hot date. I don't know why.

'Go and make some tea, darling, will you,' he said and off she went.

'Do you have to pay her to be so obedient or is it love?'

'I told you never to come here again.'

'You told me a great many things I should have ignored. Where's Louise?'

For a split second Elgin looked genuinely surprised. He thought I should know. I looked at the hall. There was a new table with curved legs, a hideous thing in maple inlaid with brass strips. No doubt it had come from the kind of shop where there are no prices but it had its price painted all over it. It was the sort of hall table interior designers buy for Arab clients. Next to it was a radiator. Louise hadn't been here for some time.

'Let me show you out,' said Elgin.

I grabbed him by his tie and jammed him against the door. I've never had any boxing lessons so I had to fight on instinct and cram his windpipe into his larynx. It seemed to work. Unfortunately he couldn't speak. 'Are you going to tell me what's happened, are you?' Pull the tie a bit tighter and watch his eyes pop out.

The hot date came tripping back up the stairs with two mugs. Two mugs. How rude. She stopped dead still like a ham actor then screamed, 'LET GO OF MY FIANCE.' I was so shocked I did. Elgin punched me in the stomach and winded me against the wall. I slipped on to the floor honking like a seal. Elgin kicked me in the shins but I didn't feel that until later. All I could see were his shiny shoes and her patent leather peep-toes. I threw up. While I was crouched over the black and white diamond tiles of the marble floor like an extra in a Vermeer, Elgin said as pompously as a half-strangled man can, 'That's right, Louise and I are divorced.' I was still coughing up egg and tomato sandwich but I struggled to my feet with the grace of an old wino, wiped my hand across my mouth and dragged its stippled backside down Elgin's blazer.

'God you're disgusting,' said the hot date. 'God.'

'Would you like me to tell you a bedtime story?' I asked her. 'All about Elgin and his wife Louise? Oh and about me too?'

'Darling, go out to the car and telephone for the police will you?' Elgin opened the door and the hot date scuttled out. Even in my decrepit state I was taken aback. 'Why does she have to phone from the car, or are you showing off?'

'My fiancée is telephoning from the car for her own safety.'

'Not because there's something you don't want her to hear?'

Elgin smiled pityingly, he had never been very good at smiling, mostly his mouth just moved around his face. 'I think it's time you left.'

I looked down the road to the car. The hot date had the phone in one hand and the instruction manual on her knee.

'I think we've got a few minutes, Elgin. Where's Louise?'

'I don't know and I don't care.'

'That's not what you said at Christmas.'

'Last year I thought I could make Louise see sense. I was mistaken.'

'It didn't have anything to do with the Civil List did it?'

I didn't expect him to react but his pale cheeks turned clown-red. He pushed me roughly down the steps. 'That's enough, get out.' My mind cleared and for a brief Samson moment my strength returned. I stood below him on the steps, below the water-line of his envy. I remembered the morning when he had challenged us in the kitchen. He had wanted us to be guilty, to creep away, our pleasure ruined by adult propriety. Instead Louise had left him. The ultimate act of selfishness; a woman who puts herself first.

I was colt-mad. Mad with pleasure at Louise's escape. I thought of her packing her things, closing the door, leaving him for ever. She was free. Is that you flying over the fields with the wind under your wing? Why didn't I trust you? Am I any better than Elgin? Now you've made fools of us both and sprung away. The snare didn't close on you. It closed on us.

Colt-mad. Break Elgin. This is where my feelings will spill, not over Louise in fountains of thankfulness but here down on him in sulphurous streams.

He started motioning to the hot date, his arms in extravagant semaphore, a silly puppet boy with the keys to a fancy car.

'Elgin, you're a doctor, aren't you? Then you'll recall that a doctor can guess the size of someone's heart by the size of their fist. Here's mine.'

I saw Elgin's look of complete astonishment as my fists, locked together in unholy prayer, came up in a line of offering under his jaw. Impact. Head snapped back, sick crunch like a meat grinder. Elgin at my feet in foetus position bleeding. He's making noises like a pig at the trough. He's not dead. Why not? If it's so easy for Louise to die why is it so hard for Elgin to do the same?

The anger went out of me. I moved his head to a more comfortable position, fetching a cushion from the hall. As I propped his crushed face a tooth fell out. Gold. I put his glasses on the hall table and walked slowly down the steps towards the car. The hot date was half in half out, her mouth fluttering like a moth. 'God. God, oh my God, God.' As though repetition might achieve what faith could not.

The phone dangled uselessly from its strap around her wrist. I could hear the crackly voice of the operator 'Fire Police Ambulance. Which service do you require? Fire Police Ambulance. Which . . .' I took the phone gently. 'Ambulance. 52 Nightingale Square, NW3.'

When I got back to my flat it was dark. My right wrist was badly swollen and I was limping. I put ice into a couple of carrier bags and Sellotaped them around my gammy limbs. I wanted nothing but sleep and I did sleep on the dusty unchanged sheets. I slept for twenty hours then got a cab to the hospital and spent almost as long in the Outpatients Department. I had cracked a bone in my wrist.

In plaster up to my elbow I made a list of every hospital that had a cancer unit. None of them had heard of Louise Rosenthal or Louise Fox. She was not undergoing treatment anywhere. I spoke to her consultant who refused to tell me anything except that he was not advising her at that time. Those friends of hers I had met had not seen her since May when she had suddenly disappeared. I tried her solicitor for the divorce. She no longer had a contact address. After a great deal of difficulty I persuaded her to give me the address she had been using during the case.

'You know this is unethical?'

'You know who I am?'

'I do. And that is why I am making an exception.'

She disappeared to rustle among her files. My lips were dry.

'Here we are: 41a Dragon St NW1.'

It was the address of my flat.

I stayed in London for six weeks until the beginning of October. I had resigned myself to charges being brought against me for whatever damage I had done to Elgin. None came. I walked over to the house to find it shuttered. For reasons of his own I wouldn't be hearing from Elgin again. What reasons when he could avenge himself on me, possibly with a prison sentence? It horrifies me to think about that madness, I've always had a wild streak, it starts with a throbbing in the temple and then a slide into craziness I can recognise but can't control. Can control. Had controlled for years until I met Louise. She opened up the dark places as well as the light. That's the risk you take. I couldn't apologise to Elgin because I wasn't sorry. Not sorry but ashamed, does that sound strange?

In the night, the blackest part of the night, when the moon is low and the sun hasn't risen, I woke up convinced that Louise had gone away alone to die. My hands shook. I didn't want that. I preferred my other reality; Louise safe somewhere, forgetting about Elgin and about me. Perhaps with somebody else. That was the part of the dream I tried to wake out of. None the less it was better than the pain of her death. My equilibrium, such as it was, depended on her happiness. I had to have that story. I told it to myself every day and held it against my chest every night. It was my comforter. I built different houses for her, planted out her gardens. She was in the sun abroad. She was in Italy eating mussels by the sea. She had a white villa that reflected in the lake. She wasn't sick and deserted in some rented room with thin curtains. She was well. Louise was well.

Characteristic of the leukaemic body is a rapid decline after remission. Remission can be induced by radiotherapy or chemotherapy or simply it can happen, no-one is sure why. No doctor can accurately predict whether the disease will stabilise or for how long. This is true of all cancers. The body dances with itself.

The progeny of the stem cell stop dividing, or the rate radically slows, tumour growth is halted. The patient may no longer be in pain. If remission comes early in the prognosis, before the toxic effects of the treatment have battered the body into a wholly new submission, the patient may feel well. Unfortunately, hair loss, skin discoloration, chronic constipation, fever and neurological disturbances are likely to be the price for a few months more life. Or a few years. That's the gamble.

Metastasis is the problem. Cancer has a unique property; it can travel from the site of origin to distant tissues. It is usually metastasis which kills the patient and the biology of metastasis is what doctors don't understand. They are not conditioned to understand it. In doctor-think the body is a series of bits to be isolated and treated as necessary, that the body in its very disease may act as a whole is an upsetting concept. Holistic medicine is for faith healers and crackpots, isn't it? Never mind. Wheel round the drugs trolley, bomb the battlefield, try radiation right on the tumour. No good? Get out the levers, saws, knives and needles. Spleen the size of a football? Desperate measures for desperate diseases. Especially so since metastasis has often developed before the patient sees a doctor. They don't like to tell you this but if the cancer is already on the move, treating the obvious problem, lung, breast, skin, gut, blood, will not alter the prognosis.

I went to the cemetery today and walked amongst the catacombs thinking of the dead. On the older graves the familiar skull and crossbones bore on me with uncomfortable gaiety. Why do they look so pleased, those grinning heads robbed of any human touch? That skulls should grin is repellent to us who come with dark flowers and mournful sober faces. This is a mourning ground, a place of silence and regret. For us, overcoats against the rain, the grey sky and the grey tombs together oppress. Here is the end of us all, but let's not look that way. While our bodies are solid and resist the slicing of the wind, let's not think of the deep mud or the patient ivy whose roots will find us out.

Six bearers in long coats and white scarves carried the body to the grave. To call it a grave at this stage would be to dignify it. In a garden it might be a trench for a new asparagus bed. Fill it with manure and plant it out. An optimistic hole. But this is not an asparagus bed, it is the last resting place of the deceased.

Observe the coffin. This is full oak not veneer. The handles are solid brass not lacquered steel. The lining of the coffin is raw silk padded with seabed sponge. Raw silk rots so gracefully. It makes an elegant tattering around the corpse. The acrylic linings, cheap and popular, don't decompose. You may as well be buried in a nylon sock.

DIY has never caught on. There's something macabre about making your own coffin. You can buy boat kits, house kits, garden furniture kits, but not coffin kits. Providing the holes were pre-drilled and properly lined up I foresee no disasters. Wouldn't it be the tenderest thing to do for the beloved?

The funeral here today is banked with flowers; pale lilies, white roses and branches of weeping willow. It always starts well and then gives way to apathy and plastic tulips in a milkbottle. The alternative is a fake Wedgwood vase jammed up against the headstone rain or shine with a wild Woolworth's spray to topple it over. I wonder if I'm missing something. Perhaps like calls unto like which is why the flowers are dead. Perhaps they're dead when they're put out. Maybe people think that in a cemetery things should be dead. There's a certain logic in that. Perhaps it's rude to litter the place with thriving summer beauty and autumn splendour. For myself I would prefer a red berberis against a creamy marble slab.

To return to the hole, as we all will. Six feet long, six feet deep and two wide is the standard although this can be varied on request. It's a great leveller the hole, for no matter what fanciness goes in it, rich and poor occupy the same home at last. Air bounded by mud. Your basic Gallipoli, as they call it in the trade.

A hole is hard work. I'm told this is something the public don't appreciate. It's an old-fashioned time-consuming job and it has to be done frost or hail. Dig while the ooze soaks through your boots. Lean on the side for a breather and get wet to the bone. Very often in the nineteenth century a grave-digger would die of the damp. Digging your own grave wasn't a figure of speech then.

For the bereaved, the hole is a frightful place. A dizzy chasm of loss. This is the last time you'll be by the side of the one you love and you must leave her, must leave him, in a dark pit where the worms shall begin their duty.

For most the look before the lid is screwed down lasts a lifetime, eclipses other friendlier pictures. Before sinkage, as they call it at the mortuary, a body must be washed, disinfected, drained, plugged and made-up. These chores were regularly done at home not so many years ago but they weren't chores then, they were acts of love.

What would you do? Pass the body into the hands of strangers? The body that has lain beside you in sickness and in health. The body your arms still long for dead or not. You were intimate with every muscle, privy to the eyelids moving in sleep. This is the body where your name is written, passing into the hands of strangers.

Your beloved has gone down to a foreign land. You call but your beloved does not hear. You call in the fields and in the valleys but your beloved does not answer. The sky is closed and silent, there is no-one there. The ground is hard and dry. Your beloved will not return that way. Perhaps only a veil divides you. Your beloved is waiting on the hills. Be patient and go with nimble feet dropping your body like a scroll.

I walked away from the funeral up through the private part of the cemetery. It had been allowed to run wild. Angels and open bibles were girdled with ivy. The undergrowth was alive. The squirrels that hopped across the tombs and the blackbird singing in the tree were uninterested in mortality. For them worm, nut and sunrise were enough.

'Beloved wife of John.' 'Only daughter of Andrew and Kate.' 'Here lies one who loved not wisely but too well.' Ashes to ashes, dust to dust.

Beneath the holly trees two men were digging a grave with rhythmic determination. One touched his cap as I passed and I felt a fraud for taking sympathy not mine to have. In the dying day the ring of the spade and the low voices of the men were cheerful to me. They would be going home for tea and a wash. Absurd that the round of life should be so reassuring even here.

I looked at my watch. Locking up time soon. I should go, not out of fear but out of respect. The sun setting behind the rows of birch long-shadowed the path. The unyielding flatstones caught the light, it gilded the deep lettering, burst along the trumpets of the angels. The ground was alive with light. Not the yellow ochre of spring but heavy autumn carmine. The blood season. Already they were shooting in the wood.

I hurried my steps. Perversely, I wanted to stay. What do the dead do at night? Do they come forth grinning at the wind whistling through their ribs. What do they care that it is cold? I blew on my hands and reached the gate as the night security guard was clanking the heavy chain and padlock. Was he locking me out or locking them in? He winked conspiratorially and patted his crotch where hung an eighteen-inch length of flashlight. 'Nothin' escapes me,' he said.

I ran over the road to the café, a fancy place on the European model but with higher prices and shorter opening hours. I used to meet you here before you left Elgin. We used to come here together after sex. You were always hungry after we had made love. You said it was me you wanted to eat so it was decent of you to settle for a toasted sandwich. Sorry, Croque Monsieur, according to the menu.

I had scrupulously avoided our old haunts – that's the advice in the grief books – until today. Until today I had hoped to find you or more modestly to find out how you are. I never thought to be Cassandra plagued by dreams. I am plagued. The worm of doubt has long since found a home in my intestines. I no longer know what to trust or what is right. I get a macabre comfort from my worm.

The worms that will eat you are first eating me. You won't feel the blunt head burrowing into your collapsing tissue. You won't know the blind persistence that mocks sinew, muscle, cartilage, until it finds bone. Until the bone itself gives way. A dog in the street could gnaw on me, so little of substance have I become.

The gate from the cemetery leads here, to this café. There's a subconscious reassurance in slipping scalding coffee down an active throat. Let the bogeys and bloody-bones, raw-heads and ghouls bother us if they can. This is light and warmth and smoke and solidity. I decided to try the café, out of masochism, out of habit, out of hope. I thought it might comfort me, although I noticed how little comfort was to be got from familiar things. How dare they stay the same when so much that mattered had changed? Why does your sweater senselessly smell of you, keep your shape when you are not there to wear it? I don't want to be reminded of you, I want you. I've been thinking of leaving London, going back to the ridiculous rented cottage for a while. Why not? Make a fresh start, isn't that one of those useful clichés?

October. Why stay? There's nothing worse than being in a crowded place when you are alone. The city is always crowded. Since I've been in this café with a calvados and an espresso the door has opened eleven times bringing in a boy or a girl to meet a boy or a girl with a calvados and an espresso. Behind the high brass and glass counter the staff in long aprons are joking. There's music on, soul stuff, everyone's busy, happy or, it seems, purposefully unhappy. Those two over there, he pensive she agitated. Things aren't going well but at least they're talking. I'm the only person alone in this café and I used to love being alone. That was when I had the luxury of knowing that soon someone would push open the heavy door and look for me. I remember those times, getting to the assignation an hour early to have a drink by myself and read a book. I was almost regretful when the hour came and the door opened and it was time to stand up and kiss you on the cheek and rub your cold hands. It was the pleasure of walking in the snow in a warm coat, that choosing to be alone. Who wants to walk in the snow naked?

I paid and left. Out here in the street, striding purposefully, I can give the impression that I've got somewhere to go. There's a light on in my flat and you'll be there as arranged with your own key. I don't have to hurry, I'm enjoying the night and the cold on my cheeks. Summer's gone, the cold's welcome. I did the shopping today and you said you'd cook. I'll call and get the wine. It gives me a loose-limbed confidence to know you'll be there. I'm expected. There's a continuum. There's freedom. We can be kites and hold each other's string. No need to worry the wind will be too strong.

Here I am outside my flat. The lights are out. The rooms are cold. You won't come back. Nevertheless, sitting on the floor by the door, I'm going to write you a letter with my address and leave it in the morning when I go. If you get this please answer, I'll meet you in the café and you'll be there won't you. Won't you?

After the roar of the Intercity train, the slow sway of the branch-line carriage. Nowadays British Rail call me 'You the Customer' but I prefer my old-fashioned appellant, 'Passenger'. Don't you think 'I glanced at my fellow passengers' has a more romantic and promising air to it than 'I glanced at the other customers on the train'? Customers buy cheese, loofahs and condoms. Passengers may have all these in their luggage but it is not the thought of their purchases that makes them interesting. A fellow passenger might be an adventure. All I have in common with a fellow customer is my wallet.

At the mainline station I ran beyond the booming intercom and the 'Delayed' board. Behind the parcels depot was a little track that used to be the only track at this station. Years ago the buildings were painted burgundy and the waiting-room had a real fire and a copy of the morning newspaper. If you asked the Stationmaster the time he would pull an enormous gold Hunter from his waistcoat pocket and consult it like a Greek at Delphi. The answer would be presented to you as an eternal truth even though it was already in the past. I was very young when such things happened, young enough to shelter under the Stationmaster's paunch while my father looked him in the eye. Too young to be expected to tell the truth myself.

Now the little track is under sentence of death and may be executed next year. There's no waiting room, nowhere to hide from the squalling wind or beating rain. This is a modern platform.

The wheezing train shuddered to a halt and belched. It was dirty, four carriages long, no sign of guard or conductor. No sign of a driver except for a folded copy of the *Sun* at the engine window. Inside, the hot smell of brakes and the rich smell of oil colluded with the unswept floor into familiar railway nausea. I felt at home at once and settled to watch the scenery through an evocative film of dust.

In a vacuum all photons travel at the same speed. They slow down when travelling through air or water or glass. Photons of different energies are slowed down at different rates. If Tolstoy had known this, would he have recognised the terrible untruth at the beginning of *Anna Karenina*? 'All happy families are alike; every unhappy family is unhappy in its own particular way.' In fact it's the other way around. Happiness is a specific. Misery is a generalisation. People usually know exactly why they are happy. They very rarely know why they are miserable.

Misery is a vacuum. A space without air, a suffocated dead place, the abode of the miserable. Misery is a tenement block, rooms like battery cages, sit over your own droppings, lie on your own filth. Misery is a no U-turns, no stopping road. Travel down it pushed by those behind, tripped by those in front. Travel down it at furious speed though the days are mummified in lead. It happens so fast once you get started, there's no anchor from the real world to slow you down, nothing to hold on to. Misery pulls away the brackets of life leaving you to free fall. Whatever your private hell, you'll find millions like it in Misery. This is the town where everyone's nightmares come true.

In the train carriage, shut behind the thick glass, I feel comfortably locked away from responsibility. I know I'm running away but my heart has become a sterile zone where nothing can grow. I don't want to face facts, shape up, snap out of it. In the pumped-out, dry bed of my heart, I'm learning to live without oxygen. I might get to like it in a masochistic way. I've sunk too low to make decisions and that brings with it a certain lightheaded freedom. Walking on the moon there's no gravity. There are dead souls in uniform ranks, spacesuits too bulky for touch, helmets too heavy for speech. The miserable millions moving in time without hope. There are no clocks in Misery, just an endless ticking.

The train has been delayed and we are sitting in

a cutting with nothing but the rustle of an evening paper and the tired stirrings of the engine. Nothing will intrude upon this passive derelict scene. I've got my feet up on the stained upholstery. The man two seats away is snoring in sleep. We can't get out and we can't get on. What does it matter? Why not relax in the overheated stagnant air? IN THE EVENT OF AN EMERGENCY BREAK GLASS. This is an emergency but I can't lift my arm high enough to smash my way out. I haven't got the strength to sound the alarm. I want to stand up strong and tall, leap through the window, brush the shards from my sleeve and say, 'That was yesterday, this is today.' I want to accept what I've done and let go. I can't let go because Louise might still be on the other end of the rope.

The station at the village is a small one and leads directly on to a lane and through fields spread with winter wheat. There's never a ticket collector, only a 40-watt bulb and a sign that says 'THIS WAY'. I'm thankful for a little guidance.

The path is bulked with cinders that give a high-pitched clink under your shoes. Your shoes will have charcoal patches and flakes of white ash but it's better than mud on a rainy night. It's not raining tonight. The sky is clear and hard, not a cloud, only stars and a drunken moon swinging on her back. There's a line of ash trees by the picket fence that takes you out of man-made things into the deep country where the land's not good for anything but sheep. I can hear the sheep munching invisibly over tussocks of grass thick as a pelt. Be careful to keep on the right, there's a ditch.

I could have got a taxi that late night, not chosen to walk six miles without a torch. It was the slap of the cold, the shock in my lungs that sent me up the cinder path and away from the pub and the telephone. I slung my bag on my back and made for the outline of the hill. Up and over. Three miles up, three miles down. We walked all night once, Louise and I, walked out of darkness as though it were a tunnel. We walked into the morning, the morning was waiting for us, it was already perfect, high sun over a level plain. Looking back I thought I saw the darkness where we had left it. I didn't think it could come after us.

I barged my way through a herd of cattle, hooves braceleted with mud. My own feet were clod-fettered. I hadn't anticipated the run-off, the slow slopes of the hill served as a drain bath for engorged springs. The rain on the dry land from a dry summer hadn't penetrated through the soil to the aquifers, only as far as the springs that fed them. They burst out in froth torrents to end in paddy pools where the cattle waded for long grass. I was lucky that the moon reflected in these waters, picking a path for me, mud-laden but not sodden. My town shoes and flimsy socks put up no resistance. My long coat was soon spattered. The cows reserved for me the incredulous looks that animals give humans in the country. We seem so silly, not a part of nature at all. The interlopers upsetting the rigid economy of hunter and hunted. Animals know what's what until they meet us. Well, tonight the cows have the last laugh. Their peaceful ruminations, their easy bodies, black against the slope of the hill, mock the flapping figure with a heavy bag who stumbles against them. Woa there! Bring that rump back. As a vegetarian I can't even contemplate revenge. Could you kill a cow? It's a game I play with myself sometimes. What could I kill? I get as far as a duck and then I see one on the pond, daft quacking, bum up diving, webbers yellow slashing the brown water. Scoop it out and wring its neck? I've brought them down with a gun and that's easier because it's remote. I won't eat what I can't kill. It seems shoddy, hypocritical. You cows have nothing to fear from me. As a body, the cows raise their heads. Like men in johns, cows and sheep do things in unison. I've always found it disturbing. What have gazing, grazing and micturating got in common?

I went to pee behind a bush. Why in the middle of the night, in the middle of nowhere, one still seeks out a bush is another of life's mysteries.

At the top of the hill, on dry ground, a whistling wind and a view. The lights of the village were like war-time coordinates, a secret council of houses and tracks muffled by darkness. I sat down to finish an egg and cress sandwich. A rabbit ran by and gave me that look of incredulity before flashing its scut down a hole.

Lights in ribbons where the road runs. Hard flares far away at the industrial estate. In the sky the red and green landing lights of an aircraft full of sleepy people. Straight below the softer village lights, and in the distance a single light hung above the others like a guiding lantern in a window. A land lighthouse making certain the route. I wished that it was my house. That having climbed to the top I could see where I was going. My way lay through gloomy thicket and a sharp plunge before the long lane home.

I miss you Louise. Many waters cannot quench love, neither can floods drown it. What then kills love? Only this: Neglect. Not to see you when you stand before me. Not to think of you in the little things. Not to make the road wide for you, the table spread for you. To choose you out of habit not desire, to pass the flower seller without a thought. To leave the dishes unwashed, the bed unmade, to ignore you in the mornings, make use of you at night. To crave another while pecking your cheek. To say your name without hearing it, to assume it is mine to call.

Why didn't I hear you when you told me you wouldn't go back to Elgin? Why didn't I see your serious face? I did think I was doing the right thing and I thought it was for the right reasons. Time has exposed to me a certain stickiness at the centre. What were my heroics and sacrifices really about? Your pig-headedness or my own?

A friend of mine said before I left London, 'At least your relationship with Louise didn't fail. It was the perfect romance.'

Was it? Is that what perfection costs? Operatic heroics and a tragic end? What about a wasteful end? Most opera ends wastefully. The happy endings are compromises. Is that the choice?

Louise, stars in your eyes, my own constellation. I was following you faithfully but I looked down. You took me out beyond the house, over the roofs, way past commonsense and good behaviour. No compromise. I should have trusted you but I lost my nerve.

I scrambled up and judged or guessed my way through the scrubland down to the lane. It was slow going, an hour and a half before I threw my bag over the final ditch and leapt across. Now the moon was high and casting long shadows on the rough road. Silence but for the sudden fox-dart in the trees. Silence but for the early owl. Silence but for my feet scuffing the gravel.

About half a mile away from my cottage I saw it was lit up. Gail Right knew I was coming back, I had telephoned her at the bar. She'd been looking after the cat and had promised to lay me a fire and leave some food. I wanted the food and fire but not Gail Right She would be too big, too present, and I felt I was becoming less present every day. I was tired from walking. My body had a satisfying numbness to it. I wanted my bed, oblivion for a while. I resolved to be firm with Gail.

The moon made the ground look frosty. The ground was silver under my shoes. Where the river ran in a thick line through the trees a low mist hung over the water. The rush of the water was bass and hard, solid deep. I bent and swilled my face, let the cold drops run down my scarf to my thorax. I shook myself and cleaved lungs with air, a hammer of cold that hit from pit to throat. Very cold now and above me a hang of metal stars.

I went into the cottage, the door was unlocked, and there was Gail Right half asleep in the chair. The fire burned like a spell and there were fresh flowers on the table. Fresh flowers and a table-cloth. New curtains in the ragged window. My heart sank. Gail must be moving in.

She woke up and checked her face in the mirror, then she gave me a little kiss and unwound my scarf.

'You're wet through.'

'I stopped at the river.'

'Not thinking of ending it all I hope?'

I shook my head and took off my coat that seemed too big for me.

'Sit down honey. I've got the tea.'

I sat down in the saggy armchair. Is this the proper ending? If not the proper then the inevitable?

Gail returned with a pot steaming like a genie. It was a new pot, not the cracked old thing that had festered on the shelf. New pots for old.

'I couldn't find her Gail.'

She patted me. 'Where did you look?'

'All the places there were to look. She's gone.'

'People don't vanish.'

'Of course they do. She came out of the air and now she's returned to it. Wherever she is I can't go there.'

'And if you could?'

'I would. If I believed in the after-life I'd throw myself in the trout-marked river tonight.'

'Don't do that,' said Gail. 'I can't swim.'

'Do you think she's dead?'

'Do you?'

'I couldn't find her. I couldn't even get near finding her. It's as if Louise never existed, like a character in a book. Did I invent her?'

'No, but you tried to,' said Gail. 'She wasn't yours for the making.'

'Don't you think it's strange that life, described as so rich and full, a camel-trail of adventure, should shrink to this coin-sized world? A head on one side, a story on the other. Someone you loved and what happened. That's all there is when you dig in your pockets. The most significant thing is someone else's face. What else is embossed on your hands but her?'

'You still love her then?'

'With all my heart.'

'What will you do?'

'What can I do? Louise once said, "It's the clichés that cause the trouble." What do you want me to say? That I'll get over it? That's right, isn't it? Time is a great deadener.'

'I'm sorry,' said Gail.
'So am I. I'd like to be able to tell her the truth.'

From the kitchen door Louise's face. Paler, thinner, but her hair still mane-wide and the colour of blood. I put out my hand and felt her fingers, she took my fingers and put them to her mouth. The scar under the lip burned me. Am I stark mad? She's warm.

This is where the story starts, in this threadbare room. The walls are exploding. The windows have turned into telescopes. Moon and stars are magnified in this room. The sun hangs over the mantelpiece. I stretch out my hand and reach the corners of the world. The world is bundled up in this room. Beyond the door, where the river is, where the roads are, we shall be. We can take the world with us when we go and sling the sun under your arm. Hurry now, it's getting late. I don't know if this is a happy ending but here we are let loose in open fields.